Kudzu

Hello Julie,

Congratulations on your
Goodreads win!

Enjoy,

Stacey Osbeck

Author photo by Erika Osbeck

Published by Wildest Dreams

ISBN: 978-0-9600507-3-4

1

Something seemed amiss as Mrs. Edwards walked
through her front door. The girls were supposed to be over
their cousins' house until late. The door was unlocked, but
everyone's door was unlocked. That's why people lived in
small towns. Everyone knew everyone. Everyone could
trust everyone.

"Girls, are you home?" Mrs. Edwards called out. No
answer. From the front door of her compact two story she
saw all the chairs pulled out from the table. Maybe she
hadn't noticed it before. It was probably fine. Passing into
the dining room, she shot a sideways glance at the gap
between the wall and the back of the china cabinet, to the
black barreled rifle. She never wanted to touch the thing
unless she had to.

She walked around the table pushing the chairs back
into position. The sound of wooden legs scraping against
the floorboards gave way to something more subtle, a soft
sound, a murmur of movement from the kitchen. Mrs.
Edwards looked over her shoulder to see a pot of water

boiling stovetop. She rushed in to turn it off. Only then did a gasp escape her lips. Awestruck, she stopped dead in the middle of the kitchen. The wooden cabinets stood open, most of their contents on the olive counters. Sugar, flour, cereal and spices all laid out before her.

Why was her kitchen ransacked? What were they looking for? And most importantly, were they still here? Mrs. Edwards snatched a long blade from the knife block and spun around.

"Who's there?" she yelled, inching backwards toward the stove. One handed, she turned the gas knob off, then grabbed a dishtowel to shift the boiling water to a back burner. Unbeknownst to her, the cloth got in the way and began to smolder the second she left the room.

Holding the knife pointing up, not sure how to handle it, she ascended the staircase. With each step the thumping in her chest grew faster and she heaved air in and out as if there wasn't quite enough. Maybe it was her own children. Maybe the girls had come home early. That was it. They were playing a prank, she thought.

"Girls, are you home?" she called out. She paused, waited for a voice, a breath, something. Nothing came.

Past the top step her feet refused to move. All three doors, the bathroom and two bedrooms, stood open. Mrs. Edwards' bed had been slept in, the blankets rumpled and unmade. Only she and her two girls lived there, but in the bathroom, the toilet seat was up.

A flicker of brightness jolted her. What was that? It flashed again, a reflection of light off the shaking blade in her hand. That's when she realized she was trembling.

"You have no right to enter a home that isn't yours!" she yelled. Her shout was met with an ear piercing screech. The fire alarm wailed! Mrs. Edwards let out a fearful shriek herself, dropped the knife and bolted to the kitchen.

The encompassing gray haze clouded visibility. Nothing was clear, except a bright orange flame that danced stovetop. Without thinking, she ran to it and swatted at the fire trying to snuff it out. Her palm blistered and she gave a sharp cry. She grabbed the simmered pot of water and doused the blaze out. Hot water and fire hissed as they met.

Mrs. Edwards spun around, barely able to distinguish anything through the dense filter of smoke and steam, and demanded, "Who's there? Who's there?" but no one answered.

* * *

The blacktop stopped a half hour back, but the road continued on. Josh hadn't noticed. He wasn't paying much attention. Sitting behind the wheel for three waking days made him overly comfortable. More recently, his brain started to cook in the oppressive late morning heat without any air conditioning in his boxy four door to speak of.

Ditches striped both sides of the unpaved stretch. Beyond the narrow dug outs, forest sprawled. It was probably a forest. It had all the hallmarks of height and shape, except no actual trees or brush were visible. For miles the woodland looking mass stayed concealed under the tightly woven blanket of a green creeping plant that covered and contained all in its reach.

A diner sign rose up with the road ahead and Josh pulled off. With the parking lot devoid of painted lines, he came to a stop in a random way near the front entrance.

Stickers of garage bands he didn't know still decorated his back bumper from the vehicle's previous owner. A patch of rust ate a hole in the metal just above the arc of his front left tire. The car lacked any special features, but took him where he needed to go. It was black, which wasn't Josh's favorite color as much as his usual default color. A large portion of his wardrobe was black including his thick rimmed glasses that he loved because he thought they made him look like a writer or beat poet of some sort.

A brass bell on a spring jingled when Josh walked through the door. The diner hadn't been remodeled since the '60s and offered a welcoming feeling of a different time. Red and white vinyl booths hugged the windows. Past a row of eight stools ran a counter of shimmery red, akin to a fancy bowling ball.

Three men ate at the counter. An older red bearded man in a green John Deere cap sat apart from the other two, on the last stool near the wall, reading the paper. He probably spent a good part of his life in that exact spot perusing the local news. All three wore plaid shirts, mesh back baseball caps and dirty workman's boots. Josh felt that these outfits were not worn in irony.

In a single swift motion, Josh lost his footing and flailed his arms in what seemed like a flamboyant dance move. He looked back at the wet patch and his cheeks got hot.

The waitress behind the counter covered her mouth in shock, or to suppress laughter, he couldn't tell, and said, "I'm so sorry. We mopped." Josh said nothing and took a seat at the counter, his eyes filled with annoyance and indignity. "I thought everything was dry so I took the sign away."

The waitress dropped her hands away from her mouth. This revealed a small hairline scar from her lip to the base of her nose where a cleft lip might have been repaired long ago. It was barely noticeable, but Josh noticed. Her blonde ponytail had come loose and short

4

wisps of hair framed her face. Her pale blue uniform zipped up the front with the V of the neckline ending in the little white pull tab of the zipper. A simple white rounded apron, tied around her waist, held pens and a cloth she'd tucked at her hip. She had those big brown doe eyes he always found sweet on girls.

"Coffee and the check please," Josh said as he spread his map of Mississippi smooth over the sparkle flecked, red counter.

"A check? You just got here."

"I'm only passing through."

The waitress placed a napkin, spoon and porcelain pitcher of milk near his map. She returned a moment later with a coffee cup in a matching saucer. Reaching for the milk, Josh caught a glimpse of the nametag pinned to her pale blue dress, just under the collar: Wendy. She followed his eyes and touched the tag briefly.

"Oh, I'm Wendy, nice to meet you."

"Hi, Josh," he said, more sheepishly than he intended.

"Where you headed?"

"Baton Rouge."

"I never been to Louisiana. What's going on there?"

"A one week writing intensive: *How to Craft a Mystery*. My favorite author's teaching it."

"Do you write mysteries?"

"Not in a while. I want to, but I never find the right inspiration."

"I only wrote when I had to. I just graduated high school."

"Me too, a month ago."

"And look at you, already off and running."

She had a warm demeanor about her and Josh felt

shy all of a sudden. He turned his attention back to the map.

"I started somewhere here…" Josh indicated a vague area off the map, somewhere northeast, "…and I need to wind up here." His finger trailed diagonally across Mississippi ending in the lower left, off the map.

Wendy placed her finger on a spot of sprawling green, "You're here now."

"I'm not where I'm supposed to be. There's not even a town listed."

"We're real small here and there's nothing nearby. You're less than two hours away though, don't worry," Wendy said. "So, Baton Rouge is where you'll be going to college? LSU?"

"I'm uh, not going to college. I was, but now I'm, um, I'm taking this one college course and seeing how things go." He pushed his dark rimmed glasses up the bridge of his nose and returned to the map.

A couple seats down from Josh, two big strong locals stood to leave. One loudly blew his nose in a tissue and tossed it onto the counter.

"Clive, I know you're not thinking of leaving that there," Wendy called over.

"Too proud to bus your own tables?" Clive said.

"There's a difference between dishes and something you blew your nose in. I'm not your maid."

Josh chimed in, "You really shouldn't expose her to your germs."

It only took a few steps for Clive to get in Josh's face, putting his hand on the counter to hover close. Clive was a lot bigger than Josh and had forty years of mean under his belt.

"Ain't nobody talking to you," Clive said.

"Okay, I … didn't feel like talking anyway," Josh

said.

"You being funny?" Clive demanded, leaning closer.

"I'm not funny. It's a, it's just not very respectful to the waitress. She seems to be working hard."

"Go on, Clive, out," Wendy said with finality.

Clive pocketed the dirty tissue and headed for the door with his friend.

"Better hope I don't see you outside this diner, smart ass," Clive warned. The bell on the door jingled as the two men exited.

"He's harmless," Wendy offered.

"He seems harmless," Josh said.

"You didn't have to do that."

"I'm just glad I didn't have to break out the big guns," he said, casually massaging his puny muscles. That made Wendy smile and when she did, that thin scar brought all his attention to her lips. Josh thought if he lived here he'd have to muster up the courage to ask her out, just so he could get a chance to kiss her. Being friendly was part of her job description. He knew that. No one takes the waitress home with them. All the same, he liked her. And he always thought the prettiest girls were the girls who smiled.

Wendy lifted the glass dome from the pedestaled tray, cut a slice of pecan pie and placed it before Josh.

"Here, on the house. You'll be doin' me a favor. I need to know how my new recipe turned out."

"You're the cook here too?" Josh asked.

"My dad runs the place. Sometimes he lets me experiment." She slid a fork beside his spoon. "Where you comin' from?"

"New York."

"New York City?"

7

"Not really, Brooklyn."

"Wow, all that way. The idea of going so far from home is a little scary for me." The bell jingled and Josh heard the chatter of two older women as they entered behind him. Wendy greeted them with a, "Good to see you. I'll be right over." She took the cloth tucked at the waist of her apron and wiped the red sparkle counter to have something to do. "I do think about it though. I'd love to go places, open myself up to the world, let new things in."

"I wish I could be less guarded like you. Guess I'm not as open to new things. I just think you gotta be careful what you let in."

"Don't listen to me. It's all talk. I've never been to a big city. I've never even left Mississippi."

"Never?"

She shook her head.

"It's a big world out there," Josh said, surprised.

Wendy looked past Josh to the women seated in the booth, thinking she should go take their order, but instead went back to wiping an imaginary spill.

"Do you live in town there?" Wendy asked.

"Excuse me?"

"Do you live in town?"

"I don't know what 'in town' means."

"Where you live are there houses and dirt roads, or apartments and paved roads?"

Josh belted out a laugh, "New York City has millions of people. Yeah, we've got paved roads." Her face dropped. "That was funny. I can't believe you said that."

"You said you didn't actually live in the city. I don't know what things are like where you live. If you want any more coffee let me know." She left the bill and walked off to attend to the women in the booth.

"Brooklyn is a borough, a section of ... I'm sorry." Josh wished he hadn't laughed at her, but he had. He wished he had something clever to say to lighten things, but he wasn't very clever.

He sipped coffee and enjoyed his dessert looking over the spaghetti tangle of highways, streets and borders for anything noteworthy, trying to figure out where he took a wrong turn. He held his spoon against the map legend to measure. With the summer sun still high in the sky it appeared he could arrive in Baton Rouge long before nightfall and get settled, despite his little detour.

With a pen from his back pocket he inked the spot Wendy pointed out in the indistinct patch of green. This didn't offer any indication of how to get there. The map only displayed major throughways. He'd have to find his own way back. Cartographers didn't even see a reason to indicate the town existed. Josh couldn't figure why he marked the location.

It was probably the pie. He'd have to come back this way if he ever wanted dessert like this again.

Diners he frequented bought mass produced desserts from a factory that dropped them off in the morning. None of these manufacturers utilized grandma's old recipes. Someone there had to have a grandma. Each sweet came from a blending of all recipes ever written on that particular dessert with the special touches averaged out in the end. Extra sugar in the mix and a glop of whipped cream plopped on before serving acted as compensating agents for the overall lacking.

Wendy put care into her pie, baked it with love and he tasted the difference. It wasn't much, but before Josh left he'd tell her he noticed cinnamon laced the crust and she used more nuts than one usually finds in a pecan pie.

He got up and handed Wendy money and the tab.

All he could get out of his mouth was, "Your pie was great."

"Thank you," Wendy said.

"I don't need change. The rest is a tip."

"I got a tip for you too, city boy. Not all of Mississippi's roads are paved and our ditches can be deep. Take it slow out there."

"Will do."

Josh relaxed into his usual driving position, his left foot plumped down lazily on its side, his thumb resting at the bottom of the steering wheel making minute adjustments. He tried placing a call one handed, but couldn't get a signal and tossed his phone on the passenger seat to his right. Only two types of music played on the local radio stations, Country and Christian. He noticed some Country Christian hybrids, but what he didn't notice, while fooling with the tuner, was the three foot long leafy branch in the road ahead.

It happened fast. Caught off guard, Josh swerved to avoid it, yanking the wheel too sharp. In the split second he thought to turn the wheel back, the momentum already sent him through the side ditch and crashing into an old dead stump. Everything came to an abrupt stop.

Josh unlatched the seatbelt, swung open the door and made his way to the front. Steam curled out from under the hood and from the rusted hole above his front left tire. The rotten stump disintegrated on impact and except for the cloud of white rising out, the car looked fine.

There was no reason to fear it was serious until Josh couldn't start the engine. He finessed the key in the ignition and applied gentle pressure on the gas, but the car had made its decision.

      The bell on the diner door jingled as Sheriff Briggs walked in. He wore his uniform of tan and brown with a polished brass star every day and switched to plainclothes only in the late evening and for church. Over the years his heft incrementally increased. He never let the ratio of chub to muscle get out of balance and now, at sixty-one, if his uniform didn't give the idea he was a force to be reckoned with, his physique did. Sheriff took a brief stroll to share a 'good morning' with the two older women in the red and white booth before seating himself on a stool, resting his hat on his knee.

      "Elmer James, how are you?" Sheriff asked the red bearded man in the John Deere cap at the other end of the counter.

      Over the edge of his newspaper Elmer James said, "Can't complain."

      "Working hard today, Sheriff?" Wendy said, putting a cup of coffee before him without him having to ask.

      "Could say that. Mrs. Edwards had an intruder," Sheriff Briggs said in his usual slow, calculated manner. The chatter between the two women in the booth stopped.

      "Mrs. Edwards? What happened?" Wendy asked trying to hide her excitement that anything at all had happened. Elmer James lowered his paper and peered over the top.

      "Not quite clear on that myself. But he sure made himself at home," Sheriff said.

      "What'd he take?" one of the older women asked, scooting closer to the end of the booth.

      "Nothing. Not a thing. That's what's strange."

      The Campbell brothers came in for lunch. When

Wendy didn't greet them they noticed everyone staring at Sheriff Briggs and wordlessly decided to sit at the counter.

"Went through her kitchen, rearranged chairs. He slept in her bed," Sheriff continued.

"How do you know it was a he?" Elmer James asked.

"Left the toilet seat up in the bathroom."

Gasps from the women in the booth.

"Maybe it was just teenagers playing around," one of the women said.

"Left a fire burning. Fire is not playing around," Sheriff said.

"I read about this," Elmer James piped in. "Just last week, happened up in Panola County. They don't take anything. They enjoy making others afraid, terrorizing them in their own homes. I forget what they called it, but it's classified as a type of mental illness."

"I'm actually not at liberty to discuss the case any further," Sheriff said. "Only brought it up so if y'all see any suspicious characters, let me know."

"Who would do such a thing?" Wendy asked.

Sheriff Briggs still displayed that controlled manner in his voice, confident that he would get to the bottom of it and said, "I don't know, but I can tell you one thing. Can't be anyone from these parts."

The brass bell on the spring jingled as Josh walked through the door.

2

"Would you call a tow for me? I ran off the road," Josh said approaching the counter.

Sheriff and Elmer James exchanged a look. Sheriff then turned on his stool to face Josh directly. Elmer James folded his paper, set it aside and pushed back the brim of his green cap with a tap of his knuckle. One of the women shifted her body around, letting her legs dangle off the outside edge of the booth so as not to miss a thing.

There was no TV set in the diner, but the show had begun.

Josh felt the quiet. A sudden fear gripped his insides, that terrible feeling that everyone was looking at him. He pushed his glasses up the bridge of his nose and took a casual glance behind him which only confirmed his suspicions. Sheriff broke the silence.

"Must've been going pretty fast."

"Trying to get out of here," Josh said.

"Don't seem like you're from these parts."

"New York, just passing through."

Sheriff Briggs eyed him up and down, taking in his black clothing, dark rimmed glasses, and dark rumpled hair that he sensed was done that way on purpose.

"New York, is that right?"

"Yeah, Wendy warned me to be careful, but right off the road I went. Oh, oh but don't worry, I'm okay."

"Glad to hear it. Wendy, I'll be back in a little while. Gonna give our new friend..." Sheriff looked to Josh waiting for him to fill in the blank.

"...Josh," Josh said, catching on.

"Gonna give our new friend, Josh, a lift to his car and radio Johnny for the tow."

"Thanks a lot," Josh said, wiping sweat from his forehead with the back of his hand.

"Not a problem," Sheriff said.

On the way out Josh waved to Wendy. Wendy raised her hand, but couldn't wipe the confusion from her face.

Josh slouched in the back of the sweltering sheriff's car, the two of them separated by wide metal mesh. A breeze from Sheriff's open window offered a scant amount of circulation.

"Could you open my window please? The button doesn't work back here," Josh said, picking at his shirt glued to his chest with perspiration. "That's only partway. Can you open it more?"

"Where you headed off to so fast?" Sheriff asked.

"I have a class starting Monday. Thought I'd get there early, settle in."

"What type of class?"

"Mystery writing intensive. It's only a week long."

"Very particular."

"I think I have a taste for crime even if it's only in a

small way."

"You know a lot about that sort of thing?"

"Nah, I used to write a couple of little mysteries. Nothing got published though."

"Is that right? How old are you, son?"

Josh lifted his hand off the vinyl seat to wipe sweat away before it spilled into his eyes. His hand and the seat made a kiss sound as they separated.

"Eighteen."

"Eighteen? Still a teenager and yet of age. Quite a time. I got a mystery here, fell in my lap today."

"Have any leads?"

Sheriff adjusted his rearview mirror to keep an eye on Josh.

"I think so," Sheriff said.

"There's my car! Can you believe I walked all that way in this heat?"

Sheriff didn't answer. He pulled to a stop. Several yards ahead two men wearing blue overalls rigged Josh's car to a beat up white tow truck, 'Johnny's Good as New' emblazoned in orange on the side.

Getting out of the car, Sheriff shouted over, "Johnny, see you found it."

"It was hard to miss," Johnny called back. Johnny's thick, jet black hair lightened to salt and pepper at the sideburns. He wasn't large, but had a certain roundness to him.

"Bert, don't let him work you too hard," Sheriff said. The younger man gave a weak salute of two fingers from his forehead in response. Bert looked to be a teenager with a height and slenderness that gave him a gangly appearance. Johnny gestured with his hands and barked orders at Bert. From afar the two looked like a denim clad Laurel and

Hardy routine.

Too hot to move, Josh splayed out like a melted gummy bear on the backseat.

Sheriff talked to Josh through the open back window, "Someone made themselves at home in Mrs. Edwards' house today. Over on Acolapissa Drive? Want to tell me anything about that?"

"Why would I know anything about that? I don't know this town at all."

"You don't know this town? Well, maybe I can show you how we do things here."

"What does that mean?"

Sheriff Briggs tucked his thumbs into his belt and headed to the mechanics.

Mississippi in the summer introduced Josh to a new level of heat, sticky-hot-punishing heat. The sweltering trek back to the diner took a lot out of him. His eyes turned down to his shirt. Wet rings under his armpits forged a slow but determined migration to meet in the center of his chest. The temperature in the backseat lulled all of Josh's senses to shut down. He felt like a live animal in a hot oven and decided he may fare better in the open sun.

Plus, it was his car in the ditch. Josh figured he should include himself in the conversation. It was also probably a good time to dig into his duffel in the trunk and put on a dry shirt.

The door handle wouldn't work. Josh leaned over to the other door with the same result. Weird, he thought, what were the chances of both handles not functioning?

"Hey, the door won't work. I can't get out," Josh called through the five inch gap of the open window. Only Bert appeared to hear him, looking over. Josh shouted louder, "I can't leave!" Sheriff stopped talking with the other two momentarily to throw an apathetic glance at Josh. Josh didn't understand. Nothing made sense. Why would the sheriff leave him in the back of the cop car knowing he couldn't get out? Why would he ask Josh where he was going and why? Why would he question him about a local break-in?

The weight of the situation finally hit Josh.

This was all a misunderstanding. In fact, maybe Josh had leapt to conclusions himself. He tried the handle again, slamming his shoulder to the door in case it was simply stuck. It created enough of a ruckus that all three men looked over.

With a white handkerchief from his back pocket, Sheriff wiped his forehead while he headed back to Josh.

"I can't get out," Josh said.

"Johnny and Bert are gonna tow it in. You can talk to them after they assess the damage," Sheriff said through the partial opening.

"I can't leave." Josh tugged the door handle a few times to illustrate.

"I'm looking for someone who at the very least enjoys harassing women in their own homes. At the worst, well I don't know, but you are not to leave town until this is sorted out," Sheriff explained.

"I have someplace I have to be. I'm taking a college course. I already prepaid for everything: my class, my dorm. I have a meal plan waiting for me."

"As much as I'd hate to keep you from your precious meal plan, doesn't seem like you're going anywhere, anyway."

Sheriff looked to the tow truck driving off, Josh's boxy black car rigged behind and pulled by the nose. Josh flopped back in his seat, defeated.

"Could you open the window more, please?"

The sheriff station couldn't be considered more than a twenty-five by forty foot box. Upon entering, to his left Josh saw four stackable chairs lined the wall, side by side. Past that a coffee maker and mugs sat atop a dark wood cabinet. Behind the coffee maker a window let in natural light.

About hip height down all the walls were painted patina green and from hip height up a soft white brightened the room. The two colors had no edging to separate them, just a crisp line probably set with masking tape.

Vertical bars sectioned off the jail cell in the back left corner.

An organized desk held a perfect position, far enough from anyone's reach in the holding cell and close enough to the air conditioner in the window on the right. Sheriff turned on the old unit and gestured for Josh to take a seat opposite him. The AC projected coolness within five feet of it. After that tight radius was a quick drop off. Two bits of blue twine, strung to the plastic slats, danced in the breeze just out of Josh's reach.

"Am I under arrest?" Josh asked.

Sheriff Briggs shook his head.

"You can't keep me here if you're not going to charge me with anything," Josh said.

"Let's be honest. Regardless of what I want, your car is keeping you here."

"Where's the closest train station?"

"There is no closest train station."

"Bus depot?"

"This is not, what you'd call, a metropolitan area. This here's a real small town. No train station, no bus stop and no taxis. There's no motel neither. But I've got a nice room you can stay in free of charge," Sheriff explained.

The kind offer mollified Josh and he sputtered out a, "Oh, well, thank you."

Sheriff softened too now that they were on the same page. He took a clattery ring of keys from his top desk drawer, walked over to the jail cell and unlocked it explaining, "This way you can have--"

"--Are you kidding?"

"It's clean and it's free."

The room's color combo, verdigris on the bottom and white up top, continued inside the cell. But the bars themselves were cold metal, top to bottom. A metallic toilet, which lacked even a basic barrier for privacy, jutted out from the wall between two beds with flimsy mattresses covered in unbleached canvas. Hinges allowed the beds to flip up against the wall, but both lay parallel to the floor, ready for their next occupants.

Sheriff stood near the open gate waiting for Josh to come to his senses.

"Let's call that plan B. Would you take me to my car?" Josh asked, all good will dissolved.

Sheriff shook his head, "I'll give you directions though." Sheriff made himself comfortable behind his desk, took out a yellow legal pad and jotted down instructions, "Only two ways to get around here: by car or by foot." He tore the paper off the pad, and handed it to Josh with a smile. "Hope you brought your walking shoes."

The noontime sun cooked the top of Josh's head. It hung too high for the towering vines on either side to cast any merciful shade on his path. His feet enjoyed the only reprieve as he walked in a puddle of his own shadow.

Josh heard the banging long before he found the repair shop. Bramble and trees crowded together on either side of the wide, gray gravel driveway. The faded sign hung above the open garage read 'Johnny's Good as New Auto Shop', written in the same orange font as on the tow truck. Josh's footsteps on the gravel driveway announced his arrival and Johnny and Bert straightened up from under the hood.

"How are you?" Josh asked.

"How are you?" Johnny replied more like a statement.

"How much will this cost?"

"Doing the estimate now. Don't know yet."

"You take credit card?"

"This is not a mom and pop operation here."

"How long will it take?"

"Like I said, I haven't finished the estimate yet." Johnny unhooked the support rod and let the hood slam shut. "I'm on break," he announced and walked off to a seat in his office.

Josh turned to Bert, "How long will it take?"

From the other room Johnny barked, "It'll take as long as it takes!"

Josh saw him leaning back, sipping soda. Josh lowered his voice.

"You don't have to do anything fancy, just make it go. Could you get it done by Sunday?"

"Nobody works Sunday," Bert said.

"Today's Thursday. It's only midday. You have today, Friday, Saturday. Please, I have a class starting Monday. It's only a week long. I put all my money into it. All my savings. I can't get the funds back if I'm a no show," Josh pleaded.

Bert ran his thumbs up and down the inside of his overall straps, thinking. He looked to see if Johnny sat within earshot.

"I'll try," Bert said low.

"Is there a motel around here?" Josh asked.

Bert shook his head, then remembered.

"Mrs. Tupelo has a room. She hasn't had a boarder in a while."

"Is that a long walk?"

Bert looked him over. Maybe it sprang from their similarity in age or that Bert seemed good natured and didn't make a habit of judging people before he knew them. The kindness also could have been triggered by the fact that Josh had officially sweat through his clothes, pants and all, and looked too pitiful for words.

"Hey Johnny, I'm taking my break too," Bert called over.

"Suit yourself," Johnny hollered back without looking.

"Let's go," Bert said.

Josh keyed into his trunk, grabbed his black duffel bag and followed the tall teenager, all while thanking him profusely.

Mrs. Tupelo resided in a more secluded section of town. No one had come this far out to clear the woods for homes or cropland. That all embracing growth climbed the forest on either side of the road. Every so often a purple flower spike jutted out, attracting hovering bees.

"Are you getting any reception?" Josh asked.

"I don't have a cellphone." Bert said.

"Wait, what?"

"No reception. No tower's close enough. It'll pick

up again when you're a ways outta town."

Josh looked down at his phone, now useless, and tucked it back in his pocket.

They turned off the dirt road onto a dirt driveway. Branches of a single tremendous oak reached high and swung low, taking up most of the front yard.

A big as the front was, with its grassy stretch leading in to a centuries old tree, the side yards by contrast were somewhat narrow. The car path on the right of the house barely had any grass as separation between it and the woods. There didn't seem to be a backyard to speak of.

The forest and the imposing oak set the place in dappled shade, which was more than welcome in the hot Mississippi heat. The periwinkle gray house stood one story tall. Besides a loose clapboard or two, the place appeared well maintained.

Mrs. Tupelo came down the side porch to greet them before they stepped out of the pickup truck. Her need to brace herself with the railing revealed her age, despite a bubbliness of youth. She fluffed the back of her short curly hairdo and straightened her floral blouse, overjoyed to have visitors. Up close Josh saw the white looping throughout her brunette locks and guessed she was comfortably in her sixties.

Bert apologized for not calling beforehand, he realized he should have.

"That's alright," Mrs. Tupelo said. "Sheriff called, said Josh might be coming by."

"How did Sheriff know I'd come here?" Josh asked.

"Only one person has an addition built on for a renter. Not much demand."

"Do you mind if I use your phone?"

"Just inside the door, on the wall."

The bright and cheery yellow kitchen had a yellow phone to match. Josh leaned his forehead on the wall as he placed the receiver in the crook of his neck.

"Hello?" a man's voice said on the other end.

Josh picked his head up off the wall, "Rick? I called to talk to Mom. Why are you picking up her phone?"

"She's in the shower. Why are you calling collect? You need money or you in trouble again?" Rick said.

Josh hung up. He stood with his hand lingering on the yellow phone a moment before going outside.

Mrs. Tupelo sent Bert off with fresh cookies wrapped in tin foil and led Josh to the back.

"You'll see. It's nice and snug," she said.

Those same vines he saw earlier grew all over the back of the house, connecting it to the adjacent woods. Their reach continued climbing up the one story clapboard's roof.

"He just cleared this," she said in frustration. Pruning shears leaned against the house with new growth vines circled around both wooden handles. She extricated the clippers from the plant's clutches and stomped forward, waist deep, with Josh close behind.

"Can stay as long as you like," she said, trudging her way through.

"Thank you, but I have to be somewhere Monday morning," Josh said.

"You're in luck. You'll be here Saturday for the fair."

The leafy green vines between the forest and the house extended well above them. When the two reached the thick of it Mrs. Tupelo headed in, swallowed up and out of sight. He heard her snipping her way through with the shears. Afraid to enter, but more afraid to lose his trailblazer, Josh pushed on.

"There's a door to the outside so you can come and go as you like, your own bathroom." she said.

The dense foliage blocked much of the light. Josh couldn't see. His eyes hadn't adjusted and he shuffled forward, following Mrs. Tupelo by the sound of her voice.

"You know where the kitchen is. Feel free to come in and pick through the fridge or use the stove. I'm meeting a friend for dinner tonight. But tomorrow it's sherry pot roast if you're interested."

Once deep inside she didn't need the clippers. The vines appeared to build and prop themselves up on each other creating a canopy of green above. A lot more than a single pair of shears would be needed to take it down.

The path she forged led them back to sunlight. They emerged on the other side unscathed.

"What is this?" Josh asked.

"Kudzu. Grows fast, comes in, takes over."

Josh looked up, "It's trying to eat your house."

"My son usually keeps it at bay. He's helping my daughter fix up her new place. Be home any day now."

Around the corner two concrete steps led to Josh's room. A window gave him the first glimpse inside: the plain white walls, a tall wooden armoire on the far right corner and the top of a chair positioned far enough back to suggest a desk sat just beneath the window.

"You can borrow my son's bike while he's gone," Mrs. Tupelo said. She pulled back a bright blue tarp beneath the window to reveal a royal blue three speed. Kudzu had crept under the plastic sheet, curled around the frame and woven itself through the spokes. She started yanking it off.

"I can do that," Josh offered and took over stripping the tendrils from the tires. Crouched down, Josh noticed under the lip of the graying shingles was a robin's egg blue, probably the color of the whole house long before the sun and storms had bleached it over time.

Once he was inside, the temperature didn't change, it merely shifted from broiling to baking. From the doorway, the lines of the wide wood floorboards stretched straight back to the bathroom. The only interruption was the oval braided rug positioned perfectly for his bare feet when he'd get out of the little twin bed. A single frosted glass sphere in the ceiling turned on with the switch near the door. A porcelain lamp sat on the night table for late night reading.

Josh threw his duffel down where he stood, next to the desk that rested under the window. Past the desk window three pictures hung, one above the other, each no bigger than a cigar box. On the next wall, to his right, a window faced the street. The tall wooden cabinet for his clothes sat in the back corner. Kudzu blacked out the window to the left of him completely. He couldn't even see the path they had just created. No curtains hung in any of the windows.

"Sheriff told me you're a writer. What are you writing?" Mrs. Tupelo asked.

"Trying to write a whodunit."

"Oh and who done it?"

"I don't know. Haven't started yet."

"I'm so glad there's a typewriter for you," she said pointing out the black keyed Smith Corona on the desk. "No one's used it in a while."

"A typewriter," Josh remarked kindly to her completely out of date amenity.

"Let me check on something. Be back in two shakes of a lamb's tail," she said heading out the door.

Sweat trickled down Josh's back, absorbing into his

already soaked waistband. None of the windows had screens. With the oppressive heat and no circulation he couldn't afford to care about bugs coming in. And he knew there were bugs. Since he got here he'd seen clouds of gnats hovering and had heard the cicadas cha-cha-ing.

He tried the window above the desk. It wouldn't budge. The heat must have made it swell in its frame. Careful not to break the glass, he whacked around the edge with the heel of his hand, then shoved hard. After a small struggle, the window shifted. He kept pushing, stutter stepping up, until the window above the desk opened all the way.

Josh checked the contents of his wallet and thumbed through the cash, mere pocket money. He didn't anticipate this detour. He'd figured emergencies would go on credit card.

"Sorry, don't have an extra fan," Mrs. Tupelo said. When she entered Josh put his wallet away. She looked to the empty curtain rods, held in place by pressure, and remembered. "I donated the old curtains to the church's booth for the fair. I haven't finished the new ones yet. Was going to do some openwork, but I'll sew up the seams and hang them now."

Unruly azaleas outside the window that faced the front road would hinder anyone's view into his room and the top half still let in a good amount of light. The window above his desk faced a fifteen foot span of grass that abruptly ended with a kudzu cloaked wooded area. Off to the left of those woods he could see the far stretches of the lone rural lane. His third window facing the back of the house only acted as a continuation of wall in its present dark green state.

"You don't have to hang the curtains," Josh said. "I

like the light. I only need the key."

"Well, I'll look, but I don't think this door has a key anymore. Nobody locks their doors here anyway."

Josh laughed. She wasn't just friendly, she was funny.

Her expression turned to confusion. She wasn't kidding. He thought to ask her if she didn't lock her own door too, but he already knew the answer. The last room offered wasn't going to come with a key either and he didn't push, realizing he picked the better of his two options.

"You're being nice after receiving a call from the law about me," Josh said. "I know you have to be careful these days who you let in."

"You seem like a good boy. I can only imagine what Sheriff's given you a dose of since you got here, but when you're under Dolores Tupelo's roof you get a taste of good old-fashioned Southern hospitality."

"I won't forget that. No good deed goes unpunished," Josh said. She gave him a quizzical look, not sure what he meant. "Sorry, it was a joke. So…" he said, clearing his throat peering into his wallet once more, "You said you don't take credit."

"Cash only."

"Do you know anyone who could give me a couple days' work?"

3

The stables were constructed of unfinished wood. The large open barn door offered a brightness. Wheat colored stalks and husks and knotty rough pinewood gave a monochromatic look to Josh's work area. Fresh straw smelled like the first days of spring. Josh focused on that while shoveling out the old, used bedding from the stalls.

Big Boss came to the threshold, silhouetted by sunlight. Unlike Sheriff, Big Boss hadn't come to grips with the fact that he'd gained weight over the years. His girth tested the limits of his buttons while he told himself he didn't need new clothes, he'd lose the weight. He smoothed his thin comb over and called to Josh from the doorway.

"Sheriff called. Wanted to know how it's going with you."

Josh stopped shoveling and leaned on the handle, "How does he know I'm here?"

"Boy, he thanked me for giving you a job so someone would know where you were at."

Josh returned to his work with a huff.

"Told him you were working out fine all the same. When you're done with this you can take off. Show up tomorrow at seven," Big Boss shouted over before walking off, not waiting for a reply.

Josh steered the wheelbarrow out back, dumped the used bedding and returned with a pitchfork. He stabbed the blond pile heaped high, walked to the corner of the stall and rotated the pitchfork, hand over hand, until the straw fell.

Someone came in and stood off to the side, evaluating the new guy. Josh pretended not to notice, but caught a glance, flaxen haired, probably his own age. A buzz cut growing in was still too short for him to style. He had farm boy good looks and a muscular build of universal appeal such as the type to be found in a calendar titled *Hot Farm Boys*. He would be draped over a tractor and have a piece of hay casually dangling from his mouth. At present, a cigarette dangled from the farm boy's mouth. He stood close enough that Josh caught a whiff of tobacco smoke. Josh couldn't figure what he wanted and pushed the dark rimmed glasses up his nose, telling himself he wouldn't let this guy intimidate him.

"So, d'you do it?" the farm boy asked.

Josh exhaled, exasperated, and said, "I've always wanted to harass women and pitch hay. Now I'm living the dream."

"Gotta respect a man with vision," the farm boy said. He took a seat on a cubed bale of straw and continued smoking. "Plan on staying long?"

"The second my car is done, I'll be nothing but a memory to you people," Josh said.

"A memory? Keep dreamin'. I don't even remember your name."

"I'm--"

"--I know your name."

Josh stopped working, giving his arms a quick break.

"I guess you're Christian," Josh said. The farm boy evaluated him, not sure how he knew. "Unless there's someone else who needs to be told not to smoke in the barn," Josh added, pointing out the bold print 'NO SMOKING IN THE BARN' sign that someone added by hand in magic marker 'This means you Christian!'

A wry smile crossed Christian's face, "Going to get a bite. Wanna come?"

"I have to finish these stalls."

Christian snuffed out the cigarette on the bottom of his shoe and tossed it in the new bedding.

"Hey!" Josh said, "What are you trying to start a fire?"

"It won't catch. Straw's too young."

"But don't you think--"

"--Shut it," Christian said.

When Josh watched him use the long handled tool he understood how the pitchfork got its name. Instead of walking the straw over and turning the handle, Christian pitched it, hurling it in a wide arc, moving twice as much as Josh in half the time. Josh mimicked Christian's movements, which proved far more efficient. They scattered the bedding evenly and tucked it along the sides.

"Done. Let's go," Christian said.

They drove in Christian's pickup, the windows rolled down, Josh's borrowed bike in the back. The radio sang of lost loves and hope of rekindling them again. Josh noticed Christian's physique and now understood it wasn't because he went to the gym. Josh filed paperwork back home and never had a manual labor job where his muscles felt taut and strong at the end of the day. He wouldn't admit it, but it was interesting trying on a new life for a time.

Out the window, the sun lingered along with the heat. The elevated road lent itself to a three foot higher view of the world. Sweeping fields of white rushed past on either side.

"Why is this road so high?" Josh asked.

"When the river feels like flooding, a few good feet above ground level can buy people time. Get outta town. My older brother worked on this here road years back. They dug out the ditches and piled the dirt up high on the road. Elevated roads like this get some asphalt. They did it in the fall so men wouldn't pass out. Can you imagine doing that in this heat?"

"I cannot," Josh said, hating the thought of it. Even with the windows open he could feel his back up against the seat getting sweaty, but when he looked around all he saw was snow.

"Wait, is that cotton?"

"This is Mississippi."

"I've never seen real growing cotton before."

"Someone's gotta grow it. Where do you think your t-shirts and blue jeans come from?"

Josh thought it over before responding, "China."

The cotton dwindled out of sight and the diner sign came up on the horizon.

Everything went quiet when Josh walked in. All eyes on him. The good feeling in the truck with Christian, gone. They slid into an open booth opposite each other. Two large white triangles, one on the back and another on the seat, came together on the red vinyl. Josh sat in the center of the great white diamond and ran his fingernail along the stitching where the two colors met, not sure what to do with himself.

Silence turned to murmurs. Chatter started up and life at the diner resumed. Josh breathed a sigh of relief.

"I have this unnatural fear of rejection," Josh said.

"Fear of rejection seems natural enough," Christian said.

"In this recurring nightmare I finally get the courage to ask a girl out. Everyone's looking, everyone, and I get publicly rejected."

"There's probably a general sense of disgust toward you here, but no real rejection."

"Thanks, thank you for making the distinction." Josh took a menu, tucked behind the table's condiments, and looked it over. "What's good here? Christian?" Transfixed on something beyond Josh, Christian didn't hear the question.

"Hmm, what? See that girl?" Christian asked.

Josh looked over his shoulder at Wendy, talking to a redhead. The corners of Josh's mouth turned up at the sight of her. Her blonde ponytail and baby blue uniform that zipped up the front. Her smile that made him smile.

"She's cute," Josh said.

"Cute? She's beautiful."

"Are you two friends?"

"I asked her out."

Josh turned back around in his seat and looked over the soup selection.

"Turned me down flat," Christian added.

"What'd she say?"

"Which time?"

Josh gave a half laugh.

"Just wants to be friends," Christian said.

"Most girls, when they meet me, they realize they don't need any new friends."

"I should give up. But she's smart and funny and I've always had a thing for redheads."

Josh turned back to Wendy and his gaze shifted to the redhead talking to her. The redhead, that was the girl Christian liked. Excitement rushed through Josh's chest. He felt surprised that he even cared. He wasn't staying. He was only working a few days, waiting for his car to be fixed.

Clive, the snotty tissue man, walked up to their booth, "Ah, the troublemakers found each other."

"Don't push your luck there," Christian warned.

"Not pushing nothing. Don't you worry yourself. You and Goldilocks have a real nice meal," Clive said before leaving.

"What does that mean?" Josh asked.

Christian scrunched his face as if he hated to, but someone ought to tell him, "They do call you that."

"Call me what?"

"Goldilocks. The Goldilocks Killer."

"The Goldilocks what? Why?"

"Tested out the chairs, slept in the bed. Boiled some water for ... I don't think I know what porridge is exactly. It's oatmeal, right?"

"I've been here five hours and I have a nickname? Nobody's dead. When did 'killer' come into the equation?"

"I know, funny, right?"

"That's fine. I don't care. I don't care what anyone here thinks of me."

"You boys know what you want?" Wendy asked. Josh hadn't heard her come over. He felt caught off guard and stared at her, mute and awkward, his mouth open hoping for the words to come. "Sorry fellas, didn't mean to keep you waiting," she added.

"We just got here. Wendy, this is--"

"--We've met. Hi Josh." She smiled, but Josh noticed she kept her eyes on her pad, pen poised, even though she wasn't writing.

"You look nice," Josh said.

"Thanks, I try to look nice," Wendy said, finally looking at him.

"I mean you looked nice earlier, but, you know, you still look nice now. Just letting you know."

"Yeah, so I'll have the usual," Christian said.

Josh nervously scanned the menu.

"I'll have the usual too. His usual."

"Be back in a jiffy," Wendy said, not needing to jot their order down. Josh watched her walk off.

"Your flirting needs work," Christian said.

"I'm not flirting. She's just a nice girl."

"So you said."

A couple rubbernecked past Josh as they made their way to the exit. Josh averted his eyes, then looked back to Christian to see how he was holding up with all the gawking. Christian didn't care. The hard stares didn't appear to bother him. Plus, he was far too engrossed with the redhead past Josh to notice much else. Josh could tell she was approaching just by the way Christian straightened up.

"Hello, Lou Ann, want to join us?" Christian offered.

"Thanks, I can't right now. Maybe next time," Lou Ann said.

She looked to Josh, and Christian said, "Lou Ann, this is Josh. He's working at the stables a couple days. Josh, this is Lou Ann, the prettiest girl in four counties."

"Stop. I have a serious favor to ask," she said, trying

to seem unaffected by Christian's flattery.

Lou Ann held a photo of a little white terrier mix with light brown ears and caramel patch around her right eye.

"She ran off. If you see her, please call me," Lou Ann said.

"You got a dog?" Christian asked.

"She dug a little under the fence and escaped."

Josh glanced out the window. That same gawking couple still stared from the parking lot and were joined by a third onlooker, the three jabbering on. Josh couldn't hear the topic, but easily guessed. He fumbled with the blinds to block them out.

"Don't worry, she's off on an adventure. When she gets hungry, she'll be back," Christian said.

"I hope so," Lou Ann said.

"What's the best way to get in touch with you? If I do see your dog."

"My phone number's on her tag. So, if you find her call me. I don't care what time it is, call me."

"I will definitely keep an eye out."

"Thanks a lot, Christian," Lou Ann said, and looked to Josh.

"Me too, definitely," Josh said, trying be a team player.

"Thanks," she said and turned back to Christian, "Maybe I'll see you again at the fair?"

"Yeah, I don't work Saturdays. I might head on over there."

"Anyway, you both enjoy your dinner." She gave a pained smile and left.

Christian watched her walk off. Josh turned to see Lou Ann's bouncy red locks sway as she left.

"Your flirting needs work," Josh said.

"Just shut it."

Josh yanked his borrowed bike from the back of the pickup. Christian got in the driver's seat. They talked through his open window.

"Sure you don't want a lift?" Christian asked.

"It's not far," Josh said, steadying the bike.

"See you at work tomorrow."

"Before you go ... why are you being nice to me?"

Christian thought it over before offering, "Everyone here hates you."

"Yeah!"

Christian turned the ignition on and flashed his winning smile, "I never follow the crowd."

4

Dark, ominous clouds rolled in. The air felt heavy and humid. Josh pedaled furiously in an attempt to outrun the coming rain. Headlights lit him from behind and he moved to the left to get out of the way. Bert, the tall thin mechanic, pulled beside him in his pickup truck and Josh slowed to a stop.

"Hey, I was looking for you," Bert said, relaxing his elbow out the window.

"My car's fixed?" Josh asked.

"I don't know you, but thought I'd do you a favor anyhow."

With a wisp of hope Josh said, "My car's nearly fixed?"

"You're car ain't getting fixed."

"Wait, what?"

"Sheriff Briggs called Johnny over at the 'Good as New' and, well, until he finds out what went on in the Edwards house, you're staying put."

Josh stood completely still, dumbfounded, straddling

the royal blue three speed. The stables, Mrs. Tupelo's room, the hawk-eyed Sheriff, all of it was supposed to be temporary until his engine turned over and took him to his weeklong writing intensive. That was what he thought at least. He couldn't imagine what his next move should be. A crackle in the distance turned his attention to the coming storm. Neither of them said anything. There was nothing to say. It was, it seemed, out of their hands.

"I'm sure something will come up," Bert added, trying to stay positive. He offered Josh a ride, only to have him decline.

Josh stood in the doorway of his room, really looking at it now that he may have to stay a spell: the dark wide wood floorboards that went with all the dark wood furniture in the room, the compactness which city living had made him used to.

A quilt of tiny apricot and navy squares with the odd floral calico here and there lay folded at the foot of his bed. He recognized the same fabrics mirrored in the oval rag rug. Mrs. Tupelo had spoken of sewing. She probably made the quilt and then fashioned the mat from its scraps.

Coming around to his desk, he placed his hands on the chair back, looking at the three pictures to the left of the window. Wire from the backings, slipped over slender nails, created an inverted V above each. He'd seen the frames when he first rented the room, but hadn't looked at the art: in the top one stags leaping and beneath it a gray skied scene with women hanging bed linens on a windy day. The last frame Mrs. Tupelo must have popped out the painting to put a kid's drawing in. That third picture depicted a crayoned sunshine and bluebirds flying with their friends. With the same bright waxed color used for the sun, the artist scribbled his name at the bottom right, *AAron,* both a's capitalized, *age 4.*

Josh took a seat and dug around in his black duffel for his bigger notebook. He packed two, a pocket sized one for musings and an eight and a half by eleven for school. He pushed the typewriter back to make room and opened to the first page. Then ran the heel of his hand along the seam to keep the cover from closing. He stared at the empty white page, hoping for inspiration to come.

He'd been here before, felt the failure before beginning. But this time everything seemed surreal: the strange turn of events, the characters he met, accusations thrown at him, the mind baking heat and outside, a volatile storm festering in the clouds.

A flash of lightning lit up dozens of silver circles on the typewriter. Josh had never really touched one before. He reached out and brushed his fingertips over the black keys. They gave under the light pressure. The typebars bulged and he heard a shifting of the mechanics within.

In the desk drawer a neatly stacked ream of paper waited. Josh dropped the pad and pen into his bag and pulled the typewriter back into position. The workings of the machine were apparent. A clean white sheet slipped in the back and the roller helped get it queued up and ready.

Each black circle, ringed in chrome, had a letter waiting to be punched. But which letter? Where to begin? A breeze came in from the impending storm. On the horizon, a skeleton of bright lightning lit up the distant night. After a silent count of seven, a rumble, then *ba-boom*! Thunder, rain—and an idea. The keys began clicking.

```
It was a dark and stormy night.
The whole world writhed, draped in
```

blackness. On the sloping landscape one lone set of headlights snaked uphill.

Wind thrashed the towering trees, swaying them violently on either side of the road. Some swung in one direction only to have the other side resile back from the force, creating a tunnel of dark movement for the automobile to press on through.

Besides the headlights, no other illumination was provided to the driver except sporadic flashes of lightning briefly giving an idea of shapes and outlines like a shadow puppet show.

Detective J. Josh did not like shadow puppet shows. He did not like driving in the rain either.

Time and the storm were not on his side. If dirt roads turned to mud his tires and journey may come to a halt. Apprehension grew. He couldn't tell if he was on the right course. Stopping to look at the map seemed risky and he threw it down on the passenger seat to his left.

Perhaps getting a [whatever a British model T was called] was a mistake. Had he received the call to solve this same mystery several months ago he would have taken a train and been collected by the chauffeur at the station.

Living in London, he never owned a horse. He hailed a carriage when

needed. Now, for the first time,
instead of someone else taking him where
he needed to go, the detective sat in
the driver's seat.

A sheer cliff stretching high
replaced the woods on the left side of
the road. To his right the forest fell
away. A steep drop thinned out the
trees with only the strongest of them
able to hold fast.

The headlights were not bright
enough. The detective only barely saw
the monstrous thing as he crashed into
it. A limb of epic proportions blocked
the road. The leafy mass reached the
height of a circus tall man and measured
about two apple carts in length. The
storm must have felled it.

After spitting out a few popping
sounds and a hiss the engine stopped.
Detective Josh cracked his door ajar.
He jabbed his umbrella through and
opened it before emerging into the
downpour.

Pushing through branches and
shining his torch around, he tried to
assess the damage. The bumper had taken
a blow and one of the headlights had
been bashed dark. Neither appeared
dire. Regardless, the engine had made
its decision.

Detective Josh gathered his map and
loose personal effects, sliding them
into his black overnight bag. After

maneuvering around the limb, he looked out into the darkness, the sloping hills and trees of the valley below. A sudden flash from above reflected off the wet, turning everything for a second stark silvery white.

He saw no refuge from the elements on the road ahead and the gales had taken a turn towards the dangerous. The car, dry and warm, rested mere paces behind. Before him an arduous trek awaited with the conditions less than favorable and the possibility that from the onset he was not headed in the right direction. As alluring as the choice to sit in a dry automobile was, mysteries were not solved by people who sat and waited in [whatever a British model T was called].

Detective Josh checked his pocket watch and marched forward. A distant burst of lightning traced the undulating landscape. In that instant the detective saw the estate house on the adjacent hill, far above the surrounding forest.

With his umbrella held close, he turned the collar up on his long black coat, pushed the wire rimmed spectacles up the bridge of his nose and trudged forward to the mansion high on the hill.

He held his umbrella so close the whole way he hadn't noticed he'd reached his destination until the pounding rain that sounded like pebbles beating down on his umbrella stopped. A stone archway, connected to the stone wraparound porch, gave shelter to anyone exiting their mode of transportation.

Upon arrival his pocket watch revealed the walk had taken a mere forty-eight minutes, despite how it felt. Although there was nothing to be done about his wet shoes and trousers he took a moment to straighten himself as best he could. Josh knocked on the front door, wound his timepiece and replaced it to his pocket.

The butler promptly answered the door. He was a strapping lad with farm boy good looks in an area of the country where there were no other good looks to be had. The detective handed him his soggy coat and umbrella which had turned inside out and back so many times it no longer could be considered useful.

Detective J. Josh entered just as he heard a car pull up on the gravel. He turned only to be blinded by the swooping headlights rounding the bend and arriving at a stop.

The chauffeur turned off the engine, went around to the back door and opened it, waiting for the man within to exit in his own time.

The chauffeur's stretched height and thinness gave him a lanky appearance, as if he were the better half of a comedic duo. From the backseat, Constable Briggs, the only lawman in this rural area, stepped out.

"Mr. J. Josh?" the constable asked.

"Detective J. Josh," the detective answered.

"Constable Briggs." They shook hands. Before releasing the detective's hand he asked, "Was that your automobile back there?"

"Unfortunately."

"That limb wasn't heavy. The chauffeur got out and moved it himself. Next time don't take it so fast."

Soaked to the bone, the detective narrowed his eyes to the comfortably dry constable. The constable took no notice of the piercing look as he picked a white thread off his overcoat. Constable Briggs had a slow, confident way of talking as if he would get to the bottom of it, but Josh sensed he was completely incompetent. The detective opened his mouth to say something he knew he'd probably regret just as his proprietor, Mr. Irons, called down from the top landing of the stairs.

"Christian! Why was I not informed of their arrival?" Mr. Irons said.

"They only arrived now, Mr. Irons," the butler replied.

"Gentlemen, have you seen the weather?"

"Yes sir, I have seen the weather,"

Detective J. Josh said.

Detective Josh watched Mr. Irons descend the finely carpeted stairs. Mr. Irons must have gained weight recently and was in denial. Surely, he could afford new attire that fit properly, but currently he tested the buttons on his waistcoat and shirt. It struck the detective as especially curious that Mr. Irons would be unaware of his appearance since he had taken great pains to artfully comb over his hair from one side of his head to meet a patch of hair on the other.

Mr. Irons thought to begin with introductions, "Ah, Detective J. Josh, so good to meet you. This is--"

"--We've met," the detective said.

"Would you like to change, sir?"

"Let's just get right down to it."

"I've some good brandy that will set you right," Mr. Irons said leading the way to the study.

The constable followed and instantly made himself at home on the leather sofa in the center of the room. Detective Josh took in the whole space before making himself comfortable.

Dark bookcases lined the entire right wall. All the shelves held important looking books it appeared no one ever read. All the shelves except for one, which housed a long glass case. A matching case sat opposite it, elevated on a stand behind the leather couch. Straight back, the far wall had two French doors leading to a stone patio outside. The detective noted the two entryways to the study: one for a stranger from the outside and one for someone already accepted into the folds of daily life. Beside the transparent doors a large window followed surrounded by numerous paintings, mostly landscapes. In the corner, Mr. Irons busied himself behind the bar pouring the first of three snifters.

"None for me, thank you," Detective Josh said.

Mr. Irons looked up surprised.

The constable looked to Josh in shock, "Truly, sir, you won't find better brandy anywhere."

"It is the best brandy one can buy," Mr. Irons added. The detective put his hand up kindly to say no thank you.

Past the bar in the corner, the next wall held a stone fireplace sandwiched in between two large windows. The fire danced warm and bright. One of the servants must have kept it stoked for the late night arrivals. In the corner to his left sat a large desk with a green hooded lamp. The main light in the room came from the overhead of five frosted glass orbs suspended from brass bowed arms. Beneath it lounged the constable on the great leather couch. Two club chairs on either side matched the sofa in hue and decorative furniture tacks.

Mr. Irons handed off a brandy snifter to Constable Briggs and took a seat in the farther of the two cushioned chairs. Detective Josh noticed that although the seating appeared arranged for ease in conversation among guests, the chair Mr. Irons sat in looked to be the only piece worn from repeated use. Josh wondered how many countless nights Mr. Irons sat in that chair alone, enjoying his brandy near the fire.

Neither of the French doors nor any of the windows had curtains or coverings. Perhaps this far out in the country the only one to peek in may be the odd stray sheep.

Detective J. Josh walked to the glass doors and looked around the floor.

"I see no sign of forced entry. Have you replaced the glass already?" the detective asked.

"Oh no, no nothing was broken. The doors were left unlocked," Mr. Irons said.

"Who leaves a door to the outside unlocked?"

"The maid swept the patio and forgot to lock it after."

"What is the name of this maid?"

"Wendy."

Josh walked to the curio cases to get a better look. The glass enclosure on the shelf contained an extensive pocket watch collection, perfect circle after circle, each placed just so. Some of the timepieces were rather old, some newer with embellished details: stags leaping, flowers blossoming, mallards flying. It was a thorough compilation and had an overall appealing look with the multitude of circlets centered between the rows of rectangular books.

The case directly behind the couch displayed a more eclectic assortment: pink fingers of coral dipped in gold, a monkey skull, a small box with silver filigree, and not one but two small portraits of Mr. Irons himself. Then there was a blank spot where something should be, but was not.

No lock secured the case, only a small latch. Detective Josh leaned in to examine the glass.

"I'm glad the two of you were able to come so quickly. With both of you on the case I'm sure it'll be solved by, shall we say, tomorrow?" Mr. Irons speculated.

"That's not quite how it works, sir," the detective said.

"I'm certain I'll find the scoundrel by tomorrow," Constable Briggs chimed in. "Although I don't see why you need the detective. I could do it myself."

Josh disregarded him altogether, "I see no fingerprints."

"Fingerprints?" Mr. Irons said.

"Has this case been wiped?" Detective Josh rephrased, standing up straight and smoothing his wet lapel.

"The maid cleaned the glass before anything was discovered out of sorts."

"The same maid who left the door unlocked?"

"The same."

"What was her name again?"

"Wendy."

Josh leaned back down almost pressing his nose to the glass, examining the empty section of the case.

"Wendy," he repeated to himself. The detective began to see a pattern. The answer to all his questions appeared to be Wendy.

Constable Briggs raised his glass to his lips, but Mr. Irons made a welcoming move with his hand for the detective to join them even if he did not wish to partake. The constable halted his motion, unsure if he should wait. When the detective put his hand up to say no thank you Briggs took that as the go ahead to start drinking.

Detective Josh got the sense that he was the only one taking this seriously.

"So this is the scene of the

crime," the detective remarked, still standing between the glass cases.

"It is. Right here the bandit snuck in and stole it," Mr. Irons said.

"Stole what exactly? You were very hush hush in the telegram, but now I'm here. What is the big secret?"

Mr. Irons leaned back in his leather chair. Still holding the brandy snifter, he rested the base of it on his thigh and fixed unwavering eyes on the detective.

"You've heard of the Iris of India?"

"...You hired a private detective to find a children's book?"

"No, no! There was a fable written of it. But unlike other fanciful stories, this one was real," Mr. Irons explained. Josh came around to the fire to dry his clothes and warm his hands. "The item taken was the Iris of India— the great sapphire itself."

"What is its value?"

"Priceless, of course. Even without the history, the size alone. Regardless, it has more sentimental value to me than to anyone else in the world. The story inspired me in youth and now look at all I have." Mr. Irons made a sweeping gesture indicating his plush study before them.

"Indeed," Constable Briggs remarked.

"Do you recall the story?"

"Refresh my memory," the detective said.

"A young British man of meager means had dreams bigger than his circumstances. He found love in the heart of a girl of some property named Iris, but her father would not bless a marriage to such a pauper. So the young man traveled to India to build his fortune.

"He worked unbearably hard day and night. All the while the two sweethearts never stopped exchanging letters. After eight long years the man had built enough of a fortune to return home to England. On his last day in India he decided to take an early evening stroll and for once look around the country he'd toiled in so long, but never taken a moment to enjoy. He heard cries for help from a ravine and discovered an Indian boy who had fallen deep down in the blackness and could not climb out on his own. The man worked his way down the nearly vertical wall utilizing the thick jungle vines that grew everywhere.

"'Thank you. Thank you,' the young boy said. 'I've been down here since last night. When the sun began to set again I had almost given up hope.'

"'Not to worry. I'll take you home,' the man said.

"The boy grabbed on piggyback and the Englishman scaled the steep slope back up from where he had started.

"Birds stopped singing, retiring for the evening. Their waning music cued the insects who began chirping.

"As they walked together the boy asked, 'What would you like as a reward?'

"The Englishman thought him rather cute and answered, 'When I get home I will go directly to the father of my sweetheart and ask for her hand. Her name is Iris so I intend on showing up with an iris to present to her, perhaps even a bouquet now that I'm not such a poor man. I've never bought flowers actually. I don't know if irises will be in season. So unless you can provide me a flower that will stay lovely on my entire journey back I don't need anything.'

"The boy's home was far grander than the man had anticipated. Several small oil lamps warmly lit the path to the front door. Magenta silks billowed in and out of upper windows. The servant who greeted them was dressed in such finery that the Englishman assumed him to be the boy's father. The servant explained all the men were out on a search party looking for the child.

"Although the boy's mother repeatedly welcomed him to come in and relax, he had to take the first morning train out and could not stay any longer.

"At daybreak the Englishman, packed and ready, waited on the train platform. As the locomotive pulled to a stop, smoke puffed out of the top and steam floated up from the bottom, creating a dense fog of surrounding white, much like a walk in the clouds.

"From the smoke and haze the boy emerged with his father. The two were a stark picture to behold in their richly dyed saffron silks.

"'Thank you for aiding my son,' the father said.

"'It's what anyone else would have done,' the Englishman replied.

"'I would like to believe that. My son told me of your conversation. I must agree it is always the mark of a gentleman, when he is gone for a spell, to return to his love with flowers, even if he can only bring but one.'

"The father took out a cloth of raw unbleached cotton. He pulled at it and the fabric fell open to reveal a royal purple sapphire, the size fit for a queen, an iris in bloom engraved on the front.

"The Englishman returned home and wed. The children's book on the tale was wildly popular. A musical on the subject ran on the West End for a time, but did not fare as well."

Mr. Irons leaned forward in his chair, quite serious.

"Many have tried to purchase the gem from me. But I don't care how much money is offered. I have no intentions of selling it to anyone. Not to anyone!"

The detective thought to himself, I heard you the first time, and said, "I'll need a list of these people."

"I don't deal with offers myself. There is a luxury goods broker I work with in London, Mr. Smithson. I'll contact him at his office. I naturally want to find the culprit, but my priority is getting the sapphire back safe and sound. Whatever it takes."

"How many members of staff do you have here?"

"Five. Lately only four. Our head maid has been in bed with a nasty cold these past few days. You've met Christian, the butler. The taller fellow, Bert, is my chauffeur. Mrs. Tupelo, the older woman with the short curly hair, she does the cooking, and then there's the maid, Wendy."

"I would like to interview the staff immediately."

"It's quite late. The staff will all be up in three hours. Why not start then when they are fresh and can answer you fully?"

"I interviewed them each over the

telephone. They don't know anything,"
Constable Briggs said.

"Quite right. Seems redundant.
Why don't you rest and in a few short
hours everyone will be up," Mr. Irons
added.

"...I see," the detective said.
"Good night then. See you at first
light."

5

Josh heard birdsong from the forest before he opened his eyes. He woke up face down on the desk, the typewriter pushed aside to make room for his head. The rains had long passed and the first brightness of day shone in.

A slender kudzu shoot reached inside the edging of the window. Tipped with three leaflets, it lingered inches from Josh's hand. Vellus fuzz covered the lobed leaves, giving the young vine a certain glow in the predawn light. Josh brushed his fingertips against the softness.

Then all that had occurred returned to him. He snapped out of his sleepiness and flashed into action. He tore the last sheet from the typewriter and thrust the pages into his duffle bag. He counted out cash, crammed it into an envelope, scrawled 'Mrs. Tupelo' on it and weighed one corner down with the black keyed Smith Corona before rushing out.

Josh made it to a main road and jogged along, looking over his shoulder again and again. When he heard a car approaching from behind he spun around, arm outstretched, thumb held high. He only then noticed the day's new underarm sweat circles on his shirt and quickly tucked his elbow back down, waving his thumb to compensate. The sun sat near the horizon and shone in Josh's eyes, blinding him to what was coming.

The car pulled to a stop. Josh let his hand flop by his side when he recognized the vehicle.

"Hitchhiking's illegal. Good thing I was here to stop you before you committed the crime this time," Sheriff Briggs said in his usual unruffled manner.

With a jab of the thumb, Sheriff indicated for him to get in the back of the car. Josh looked around trying to figure out an alternative. He couldn't see one. What was he going to do, flee into the woods and hide out there? From what he knew of Sheriff Briggs the man would surely send the bloodhounds after him. So Josh reluctantly got in and returned to the spot he'd found himself in yesterday, sitting in the back of the sheriff's car, sweating through his clothes.

Josh wanted to say something in his defense and tried to formulate his thoughts before it spilled out wrong. Too many times when it mattered words failed him. He was already going to be locked up for hitchhiking, he didn't want his mouth to get him in any more trouble than he already was.

Sheriff pulled down a bumpy country road. It was definitely not the way to the sheriff station. Josh grabbed the wide mesh separating them to pull himself up.

"Where are we going?" Josh asked.

Sheriff said nothing.

"Where are you taking me?"

Again there was no answer. A heavy feeling pushed on Josh's chest. He let go of the woven metal and slid back, wondering if the fate before him could be worse than the holding cell.

The curved cedar archway read 'Irons Stables' with the iron letters taken to rust. Josh wished Sheriff Briggs could feel the look he was using to try and bore a hole in the back of his head. But the sheriff didn't need to see it. He already knew.

Sheriff dropped him off at work and drove out of sight. Josh stood there, his hair and clothes wet with sweat. He gripped the canvas handles of his black gym bag tightly, stewing.

He headed off to the stables when Big Boss caught sight of him and shouted over, "You're seven minutes late, mister! Do that again and you're fired! Now get in there and start cleaning the buckets!"

Josh stopped walking and didn't turn to say anything. The day had only just started, but was already looking like a hard one.

In the stable he tossed his duffel off to the side and got started. He removed the galvanized water buckets from the stalls and brought them out back, cleaning each with a brush and hose. After filling the metal pails with fresh water he walked them inside one by one. On his way to get a wheelbarrow and shovel he saw the horses out at pasture, eating and frolicking. He wished life could be that easy.

He began separating the soiled bedding from the clean as Christian sauntered in.

"I'm not trying to tell you what to do. But try and get here on time. It'll make things easier with you and the Big Boss," Christian said.

"I'm not staying. I don't even know what I'm doing here," Josh said, getting irritated and throwing his shovel aside.

"Who cares if you're staying or going? You're here

now. Make the best of it."

Big Boss walked by the front opening, looking in, smoothing his comb over. Josh picked up his shovel and started working again. Christian gave a brief nod to say hello and lit up a cigarette once Big Boss passed.

"You're gonna tell me how to be a model employee?" Josh asked.

"I'm just saying I show up on time, do my job, and follow the rules."

Josh pointed to the 'NO SMOKING IN THE BARN' sign and Christian took another drag off his cigarette.

"Why don't you shut up?" he said and grabbed a shovel and went to work in the next stall.

Christian wiped sweat from his forehead using the rolled up part of his sleeve in the crux of his arm. His plaid work shirt had damp spots on his chest near the second open button and on his shoulder blades where the fabric formed around his muscles. How did Christian make hot look so cool? Josh didn't need a mirror to know how he looked. He looked how he felt, like a drowned rat.

"Why does everyone call him Big Boss?" Josh asked.

Christian shrugged, "When his son comes 'round we just call him, Boss."

"Hey, feel like going to Baton Rouge today? I'll pay for gas," Josh said.

"Why would I want to go to Louisiana?"

"We could meet some new girls."

"I think I've almost won over Lou Ann," Christian said.

"While she's giving you the cold shoulder you're a free agent. I'll be your wing man."

"Thanks, but I prefer to fly solo. We'll miss the fair

tomorrow."

"I can live without the fair. What do you say? It'll be an adventure."

"It probably won't."

"I know," Josh said not able to pull off the possibility. "But what d'you say?" Christian thought about it. Josh added, "Sheriff thinks the home invasion was me and he's not looking anywhere else. I can't leave without your help. I'd owe you big time. My dorm room's already paid for. You could stay the weekend and we could squeeze in some good fun. Let's be honest, the mystery of the Edwards break-in is already old news. No one's gonna figure out who done it." Josh looked at him pleadingly. "What d'you say?"

Christian mulled it over, "It's Friday. Payday. Let's work double time, see if we can get our cash and get out early."

Josh knocked on Mrs. Tupelo's open kitchen door. "Come on in, Josh," she said.

Her cooking turned the kitchen far hotter than the outside, but the way it smelled Josh didn't care. Pot roast and potatoes and freshly baked bread mingled together, exuding a scent reminiscent of a homecoming.

A simple white stained glass lamp hung above her kitchen table. The milky translucent panels had yellow eyed daisies painted on. The walls and counters were a gentle yellow, not a zesty citrus, but more akin to yellow apples.

Sewing supplies and cloth lay on the small kitchen table. A wooden embroidery hoop pulled the white fabric taut. Dark blue thread finished the large eyelet flowers cut along the bottom edge.

"I got off early from the stables. Am I interrupting?"

Josh asked.

"Course not. Dinner won't be ready for another few hours though."

"I have other plans, but thanks. I was gonna grab a piece of fruit or two."

"Sit and I'll make you a sandwich. You can take it with you if you're in a rush."

"That'd be great, thank you."

She poured cooking sherry over the roast in the oven and then some in her glass.

"I never drink, but when I make my sherry pot roast I do indulge in a nip or two," Mrs. Tupelo said. She slid a tea towel off a bread pan. With two pot holders she flipped it over. A few seeds fell off the top and bounced on the counter. After shaking the new loaf out, she removed the heel and cut two thick warm slices.

Josh leaned forward in his seat looking out the window at Christian, still in his truck waiting to go.

"Where'd you learn to sew?" Josh asked.

Mrs. Tupelo glanced at her curtains in progress while Josh flipped through a book on the table titled *Encyclopedia of Sewing*.

"Teaching myself. I really want to join the sewing circle. They meet first thing in the morning, most days. So, you have to be serious to join. I've tried and, well, they won't let me in."

"Why not?"

"They can only fit eight around a quilt."

"Can't they squeeze in one more?"

"You'd think they could, but Mrs. Keets is very selective," Mrs. Tupelo said.

"What's the selection process?"

Tin foil crinkled as she folded it around his

sandwich. She put the shiny sandwich square and two small apples in a brown paper sack and handed the on the go meal to Josh.

"No one's ever quite sure," she said.

"Looks like you're doing a great job on your own."

"It's not just the sewing. The circle knows everything worth knowing in town. It's a fun group to belong to. So I've heard." Mrs. Tupelo didn't seem to want to talk much more on the matter and opened the oven to check on the roast, pouring a bit more sherry over the meat and a bit more into her glass.

"Would you like a bottle of Coke?" she asked.

"Would it be too much to ask for two?"

She took two glass bottles of soda out of the fridge and handed them to Josh.

"Enjoy."

"Thanks a lot," Josh said and headed for the door.

"Before you go, did you figure out who done it?"

Josh stopped mid step, "What do you mean?"

"Did you solve the mystery?"

"I'm not going to track down the culprit myself."

"What? So you didn't finish your story?"

"Oh, my mystery, my story. No, I didn't solve it yet. Still uh, still working it out." Josh held the brown paper bag up, "Thanks for lunch," and then walked out to his ride.

"That took about four years," Christian said as Josh got in the truck. "I coulda gone to college myself, graduated already and come back. What were you doing in there?"

"Quit complaining. I got us food for the ride." Josh handed Christian a soda and dug into the lunch sack. "I feel bad not telling her."

"You left her money in your room. You didn't cheat her."

"You don't think she called Sheriff on me about running away when I tried hitchhiking?"

"She don't know anything about that. Sheriff patrols the roads because he got nothing better to do. Woulda let you keep walking in the heat if he didn't see you trying to thumb a ride. Probably did yourself a favor."

Josh unwrapped the sandwich and gave half to his friend.

"Glad I won't have to see Big Boss again," Josh said.

"He just acts hard so people don't walk all over him. He's a big softy."

"I don't know about that."

"What do you mean? We asked to leave early without any notice and he let us go."

"Anyway, this is great."

"I know, Mrs. Tupelo still bakes her own bread. It's a shame she's old enough to be my grandma. I love a woman who can cook." Christian glanced down at his half of the sandwich with approval.

"No, I meant I wasn't even gonna go to school this year. Then I heard about this class and got a second chance."

"Second chance at what?"

"Second chance at going to school. Taking a college course."

"What happened with the first chance?"

"It's a long story."

"It's a long car ride to Baton Rouge you realize."

Josh looked out the window at the world rushing past, not sure where to begin, "There was this test." Christian looked over at him, waiting for him to go on. "Each year my high school offers scholarships to three seniors. It's based on overall grades and this one big exam.

I studied after school for that test. I studied on my lunch breaks, weekends. When the test came, got a perfect score, hundred percent. So I was guaranteed to be in the running. When I heard my name called over the loudspeaker to go to the office I figured I earned the scholarship. I remember walking through the principal's door, thinking this is it. That feeling when you put in the work and it pays off, when things finally go your way." Josh took another bite of his sandwich.

Christian had to wait for him to finish chewing before he went on with the story, "And?"

"And only other person with a perfect score was the idiot football player sitting right next to me during the test. He copied my work the whole time."

"They confront him?"

"They questioned him before me. He said we helped each other with the answers during the test. That it was my idea. Tried to skirt the blame."

"What'd you say?"

"I said it wasn't true. I studied. I worked hard and I did not give him the answers. The thing is they said they were going to expel me if I didn't admit to cheating and being a party to cheating."

"But you didn't do it."

"I couldn't get expelled. If I admitted it they wouldn't put it on my permanent record. I could graduate quietly."

"Why would you admit to something you didn't do?"

"I'd lose anyway and it would be on my transcripts. What college would take me then?"

"But you didn't cheat."

"Christian, sometimes there's the way things are and then there's the way things seem." They both ate quietly for a time. Josh looked out the window at the kudzu covered woods passing by. "That jock and his buddies, they used to … they used to pick on me. They were bigger than me. I would just brush it off. In the end, though, that jock, he screwed me out of college. I had to tell the school I had my eye on I couldn't go, not this year anyway. I didn't get enough financial aid. But when I heard about this one week intensive class, it's exactly the--"

"--You admitted to something you didn't do?"

"I couldn't get expelled from high school. No college would take me. Plus, my stepfather would kill me. You don't know what Rick's like. The second I graduated I got my own place to get away. He always saw the worst in me even when it wasn't there. Accusing me of stuff I didn't do like stealing cash from his wallet. I never stole anything in my life. Now this place." Josh grew angrier the more he thought about it. "I gotta tell you, getting accused of things I didn't do is turning into the story of my life. Got accused of cheating, was allowed to leave school quietly. Got accused of stealing, had to leave my own home. Here, I'm getting accused of breaking into people's houses."

"Well, now you're leaving so, doesn't much matter," Christian said.

The sky opened up as the towering woods on both sides dropped away and miles of even cropland spread to the horizon. Neat rows of corn went on for acres with their silk tassels catching gusts from passing cars. Farther down the road some type of blond crop grew, maybe hay or grain for livestock.

"I am leaving. Again," Josh said, more to himself than to his friend. "Wait, hypothetically, if someone wanted to bike your town, the whole town, in only a day or two, could they do it?"

"They could do it in a day, if they wanted to."

"Really? A day?" Josh turned in his seat, "Christian, I have an idea. Would you be willing to go to Baton Rouge Sunday instead?"

"Instead of what?" Christian looked to him, "Instead of now?"

"I know, I'm sorry. But could you drive me Sunday?"

"You forget something?"

"I'm not leaving this time. I didn't do it."

"Are you kidding me? We're already on the road. No one's accusing you of manslaughter. This is small stuff here," Christian said.

"Of course it's small stuff. If it were manslaughter, I wouldn't be able to go around town. I'd be locked up right now. It's always small stuff, but if I don't stop running, if I don't clear my name this time, this may just become the story of my life."

Christian exhaled all the air out of his chest.

"Honestly, you driving me right now, it's a temporary solution. When class is done I still have to get all the way back home somehow. I'll need my car. If Sheriff Briggs gets the real criminal he'll finally let the mechanics get to work. I need to at least try. You driving me Sunday would only be a backup plan. A just in case plan. It's a small, small town. Somebody knows something."

"If I considered sayin' yes to Sunday, what are you fixin' to do?" Christian asked.

Josh spoke with newfound determination, "I'm going to clear my name, solve the mystery of the Edwards break-in, and solve it with enough time to get to my class."

Christian took his eyes off the road to give Josh a good look over, make sure he was serious, "Can you do that?"

"I have no idea-- yes! Yes, I can!"

Christian slowed the truck and turned it around, "Gotta respect a man with vision."

6

Josh and Christian joked around on the ride back and wondered aloud if they could meet girls at the fair the next day with so many coming in from neighboring counties. Christian promised that if Josh didn't solve the Edwards break-in he'd take him to Baton Rouge come Sunday. Josh got the impression Christian had no faith that anything would be accomplished by turning around. But Josh remained hopeful.

Josh had a guaranteed lift to class. Furthermore, he had a chance to clear his name and expedite the repair of his car, which would let Christian off the hook for the favor. He couldn't lose.

The heat rose brutal. The humidity sealed all things to each other. A roof overhead and the open windows offered some relief, making the ride back seem rather luxurious.

Josh's mind raced with the excitement of taking the reins instead of running when trouble hit. This time things would be different. He would interview every resident.

Even if he didn't interview every resident he could talk to most.

They drove on and the terrain became familiar again. Josh recognized the landscape of vine draped woods and sporadic farmland. A rising dread swelled in him the closer they got to Mrs. Tupelo's, that fear of turning rhetoric into reality.

Talking to the whole town, even a small town, seemed overly ambitious by anyone's standards. Five would be a good round number to start with. He'd speak with five townspeople.

The thought of five made it hard to focus. Three was really a round number. Five wasn't round or even. Three was bite sized.

His whole thought process devolved and by the time Josh stepped out of the truck and shut the door behind him he was kicking himself for asking Christian to turn around at all. He had an easy out and he'd blown it.

Josh remained motionless on the road in front of his room, holding his black duffel, watching his once immediate getaway plan drive out of sight. The only emotion growing stronger than fear was anger, at himself. Who has an escape route, turns it down to clear his name, then sits around and does nothing? He wanted to tell himself not him, but his courage number had been whittled down to zero. Zero was easy. Zero was doable.

In the truck with Christian he'd given himself more credit for gumption than he deserved. What was he thinking, that he was some sort of detective?

Pans clanked in the kitchen behind him. Sherry pot roast, at least, was in his future. He liked pot roast. He still stood where the grass met the dirt road, unmoving. A familiar sense of defeat crept in. Josh hated that feeling and this time he told himself he wouldn't let it take root. For once his disappointment was stronger than his fear.

He gripped the handle of his bag tight and made a fist with his other hand. He couldn't wrap his head around five or three, but what about one? Talking to one person in town. One scared him too. Zero to one was actually a big leap.

He figured if he asked a skydiver how many times she'd jumped out of a plane she might say 'Ninety, a hundred, I can't remember.' If he questioned a beginner in the skydiving world she may say 'Six, I'm going in for seven. Once you start leaping you just keeping going.' But what would a novice say? The person suiting up, buckling into their pack, taking their first step onto the plane for their first free fall? That was the real leap, going from zero to one. Everything starts with the first time.

This was not leaping out of a plane. This was talking to people. This was doable. He'd done it before. He would talk to one person and go from there, if he felt like it. Right now he would only think about accomplishing an interview with one person. But who?

If Mrs. Tupelo had even a faint inkling of a lead she'd have told Josh already. Same went for Christian. Bert had been nice. He could talk to Bert and check on his car's progress. See if its repair still rested under the thumb of Sheriff Briggs.

Josh went back to his room, dropped off his bag and dug out a pen and his smaller notebook that fit in his back pocket. He retrieved the bike out from under the bright blue tarp lying beneath his open window.

He found his way to the 'Good as New' without making a single wrong turn. Unfortunately, Bert was nowhere in sight. Johnny tinkered with a motorcycle. The grease stains on his hands were as black as his slicked back hair.

"I wanted to ask a few things about Mrs. Edwards," Josh said. Every time he spoke Johnny revved the engine over his voice. "I was actually looking for Bert."

Johnny cupped his hand behind his ear illustrating he couldn't hear him.

"I want to--" Josh started.

Rrrrrrr!

"Could you stop that for a second?"

Johnny gunned it again and Josh walked off, aggravated.

From his treatment at the mechanics shop Josh thought it may behoove him to chat with someone he hadn't met before. He biked up to a house with an African American woman out front planting seedlings under her tree. She wore a wide brimmed straw hat and knelt on an old magazine, tilling the soil with a hand trowel. When she heard Josh's bike stop she stood and took off her floral print gloves.

"Hello, I wanted to ask you about Mrs. Edwards," Josh said still standing astride his borrowed bike.

"What about Mrs. Edwards?" the woman asked, taking a floral print handkerchief from her back pocket and dabbing her face.

"Well, she had a break-in."

"So I heard."

"I'm trying to figure out what happened. Any information would help."

"Don't know her well. She lives on the other end of town."

"Did anything seem strange that day?"

"Yesterday?"

"Yes."

"No, again, it was on the other end of town."

Josh had not thought through a solid line of questioning. The idea that he would canvas the area and some type of useful information would simply emerge only now appeared unrealistic.

"Oh, thanks, have a nice day," Josh said.

"You too," she said, kneeling back on the magazine and putting on her floral gardening gloves.

That got him nowhere. Did it count as interviewing one person? Maybe. Probably not.

Biking further down the way, he came upon an old abandoned church shrouded in green. Kudzu reached from the neighboring woods covering the whole thing, steeple tall. The broken concrete path still indicated the way to the front door. Josh wondered what the pews and altar inside looked like, if it was frozen in time from the day everyone left or nonexistent, gutted long ago.

Past the grown over church the trees and greenery stopped. Cotton, expansive fields of it, dominated both sides of the elevated road. If he wasn't mistaken, Christian had driven him this way once before. Josh stopped pedaling and put his feet on the ground. Looking around Josh could see over the cotton in both directions, see all the way to where the huge swathes of white stopped and green began again. A breeze passing over the cotton sounded gentle, softer than leaves rustling in the treetops. And for a moment, he couldn't place why, he felt good. Josh felt happy. A wonderful view surrounded him and perhaps, just perhaps, possibilities still lay ahead.

The airflow subsided, Josh got in gear and headed off.

The end of the cotton bordered a dirt road which

sloped down from the elevated street. The bike hummed a *zizzz* as he coasted down the incline where the two ways connected. A sign read 'Song Brook Lane.'

Toward the back of the white field, set far off from both the main and dirt roads, a small house with a large front porch peeked out from behind the cotton. An elderly woman in a loose fitting housedress, with a long white braid wrapped around the crown of her head, swayed forward and back in her rocking chair. A black shotgun rested across the curved wooden armrests. Her hands relaxed on it comfortably. Josh biked up the long driveway, her eyes locked on him the whole way. An older person probably had been here long enough to see what really went on and knew all the town's little secrets. He got off the bike, laid it in the grass and walked up the brick paved path to the front porch. The crotchety woman's scowl looked as though it had been stuck there for years.

Before Josh could arrive at the porch she gripped the firearm without yet lifting it and shouted, "I know who you are. Get off ma land!"

When a woman and her shotgun tell you to go, you go. Josh put his head down, pushed his glasses up his face and took the long walk back down the brick path, none the wiser.

The day grew hotter, the cicada clacking intensified and Josh noticed sweat came through on his shirt in patches, giving his black tee a blotchy look.

Farther down Song Brook Lane, Josh came upon a boy who looked about five years old. He manned a stand of two wooden crates with a board laid across. Yellow construction paper pinned to the side read 'Lemonade $1' with a simple lemon outlined beneath in black magic marker. The kid wore a cowboy hat, brown fringed vest and a sheriff's star. His business venture consisted of the yellow sign, the stand, a large glass pitcher of lemonade and two dozen small paper cups. When Josh rode up, the little cowboy sheriff smiled and put his hand on the pitcher, hoping.

"I'll take a glass," Josh said.

After turning a couple cups from the stack right side up, the boy reached two handed for the big glass pitcher. Sliced lemon circles floated amidst the melting ice. Too full and too heavy, the weight made the boy sway. Right before he poured, the spout tipped the empty paper cup over.

"Could you hold it steady please?" the boy asked. Josh put his hands on both waxed cups and the kid filled them to the brim. The boy raised a glass to Josh and they drank together.

"It's healthy lemonade," the boy said.

"I could tell it's healthy. Man, is it healthy. And strong."

"No sugar," the boy said straightening his cowboy hat proudly.

Josh swigged the rest down in one gulp. It was nice to have a quick refresher. He took out his wallet to pay, but the kid put his hand up.

"No can do. Outlaws drink free at my corral."

Josh set the dollar down, "I'm no outlaw."

Josh pedaled off down the dirt road. He sensed the kid watching. Once he felt sure he'd gone far enough to be out of sight he pulled up the bottom of his black tee shirt and wiped his forehead. The front of his bangs had turned sweaty wet sometime back.

Who wanted to get interviewed by a guy who looked as if he'd made a beeline from the shower to their front door? They'd know his hair wasn't wet from the shower.

They'd know he was sweating like some lunatic who did crazy things, like go into women's homes and engage in peculiar acts of menacing. He may inspire more confidence from others if he looked pulled together, and for a moment Josh considered freshening up in his room. He pushed that thought aside, knowing once he turned back he might not go out again. He would stick to this course and conduct at least one useful interview. One and he could call it quits.

Up ahead faint melodies floated out from an open garage. Josh took a deep breath and rode up. Long strips of bright white aluminum siding wrapped around the whole house. In the side yard bamboo teepees coaxed string beans to grow and soft stems of tomato plants bowed under the weight of the plump red bounty.

Walking to the entry of the garage, Josh didn't see anyone. A stack of cardboard boxes created a wall that obscured his view, but somewhere behind it a window let rays of light in. The tune ended. Whoever stood behind the box wall didn't like the next one and turned the radio dial for a new song: static, music, talk radio.

Josh looked overhead and saw the garage door close to the ceiling on runners. The gray concrete walls and floor made the space cooler than outside. Ambient sunlight lit the garage. A single lamp above remained off and probably wasn't powerful enough to affect the heat or light situation either way. The person settled on some boyband that Josh faintly recognized.

He called out, "Hello?" to which the radio turned off. A head popped out from around the box wall. "Wendy," Josh said, surprised.

"Josh, what are you doing here?" Wendy's blonde hair fell down just passed her shoulders. Her plain white tee had been knotted off to the side and she'd cuffed her jeans up to high waters. Her tan sandals each had a little red heart centered on the front, near her toes.

"I'm trying to talk to people, get leads on the Edwards break-in. Going around and, uh, wound up here."

"How many people you talked to?" Wendy removed the hair tie from her wrist with her teeth. She held it there while she ran her fingers through her hair, pulling it up into a ponytail.

"I got ignored down at the 'Good as New,' one woman didn't know anything, a retiree told me to get off her land and now there's you. Well, there was a kid. We didn't really talk. He just sold me lemonade."

"Who told you to get off their land?" she asked with the hair tie still in her front teeth.

"We didn't exchange introductions."

Wendy laughed while she finished tying her hair back.

Josh couldn't help laughing too, "I know. Weird."

She leaned on the cardboard boxes a moment, considering him. Some unseen window illuminated Wendy's loose blonde strands from behind, giving her face a soft halo of light.

"What you been asking?" Wendy said.

"I have a hunch. She's *Mrs.* Edwards, right? But there's no Mr. Is he estranged? Maybe he came back."

"He passed, little over a year ago."

"Oh … I'm sorry to hear that." Josh took out the notepad and pen from his back pocket and scratched that off.

"What other questions you have?"

"That's it so far."

"That's it?"

"So far. I hope you don't think I did it."

"I don't, but I'm still not sure what to make of you

either way."

"I'm an alright guy," Josh said. Wendy smiled at that, but didn't say anything so Josh clumsily added, "And I'm helpful. What are you doing in here? I can help."

"It's boring work."

"That's okay. I like boring. I'm kind of boring myself."

She laughed, not realizing it wasn't a joke.

"I'm pulling donations for the church thrift booth. You going to the fair tomorrow?" Wendy asked.

"Probably not. Are you?"

"I'm entering one of my pies in the competition."

Josh tightened his lips and nodded to himself, "Maybe I will go then. Just to watch you win."

"Thank you for sayin' that. You just warmed my heart."

Josh opened his mouth to say 'my pleasure' but shut it almost as quick, afraid he's say the wrong thing and ruin the moment.

Wendy took a cardboard box from the top row of the box wall and put it on the floor between them.

"Beulah Dawson always gets first place," Wendy said. "This year it's gonna be me." She crouched down and pulled off the packing tape. "I don't know why all this stuff got shoved in unmarked boxes." Inside, resting above various toys and dolls lay a Fisher Price barn.

"I had this too. You open the door and it moos." He opened the barn door and alas, a *moo*. "This thing was so fun. I have to tell you, real barns, not as much fun."

"Some kid'll like this. Let's find the animals."

They bent over and dug around together searching for different barnyard friends. The coarse wool yarn of a rag doll's hair and fluffiness of stuffed animals rubbed against their bare arms.

"Are you entering that pecan pie? The one I tried when I first met you?"

"That's the one."

"I think about that pie sometimes."

"Why?"

"It was still warm from the oven. The recipe seemed well thought out, not too sugary sweet. And I liked your accent. You have a little Southern twang when you speak."

"I talk like everyone else around here."

"I know, but I only noticed it with you."

"What does that have to do with pie?"

Josh's cheek brushed up against her cheek. It was bound to happen with them rummaging so close through the same box. Josh couldn't remember the last thing Wendy asked him and thought maybe he should apologize. He thought to say I didn't mean to rub my face against your face, as Wendy said:

"Cow."

"Excuse me?"

"Cow, I found a cow and one sheep."

"I'm not getting anything."

"There should be more sheep. Keep reaching. They travel in groups."

"Hold on. There's a better way to do this," Josh said. One by one he handed her the dolls, the toys and everything soft and light from the cardboard box. He touched a smooth plastic thing.

"A crazy haired troll. I had this. Mine had orange hair," Josh said, holding the turquoise haired creature.

"I think I still have an orange haired one somewhere."

Josh liked that while they sifted through Wendy's

childhood they also looked back on his own. At the bottom of the box they found the missing pieces: a horse, a dog, a rooster, a family.

"Great, would you mind putting it all in that empty box? That's what I'm donating," Wendy said, indicating the box near the mouth of the open garage.

Wendy stood up, dumping some of the toys in her arms back where they came from and the rest in the donation box. She stripped tape off another and opened the cardboard flaps. When she determined it held nothing but children's clothes she put it aside and moved on to another one.

"Kid clothes? Why don't you donate these?" Josh asked.

"These I'm keeping."

Josh held up a frilly white dress for a toddler.

"What is this? A teeny tiny wedding dress? For a five year old?"

"It's a christening gown."

"You're never gonna use this again."

She took it out of his hand, "I might."

"What are you, five?"

"My grandmothers sewed my clothes when I was young. I'm allowed to hold on to some things for sentimental value."

"That's fair. What can I sort through that doesn't involve fashion?"

"Here, books. Most of these can go." She handed him a heavy box. They each picked through their own container, making piles. She with toys and he with the books. "We're actually closer than you think," Wendy said. She stood up and dragged her cardboard box, pulling it by the flap, nearer to Josh.

Don't say anything stupid. Don't say anything

stupid.

"Oh? We're close?"

"You don't live far from me."

"I don't know about that. And if you biked in the heat today you definitely wouldn't say that."

"Not by the roads. As the crow flies, you're only about a mile away."

"*Nancy Drew?*"

"I've read those all already."

"Me too," Josh said, tossing the books in with the donations.

"Really? I would have thought you read *The Hardy Boys.*"

"I read them both."

She continued sorting through her box, "That's exciting, you trying to solve the crime."

"I'm finding it's not as exciting as I hoped."

"I'm excited. If you find out will you tell me?"

Josh looked up from the books to face her, "Of course."

"There's only thirty, thirty-three households or so within the town limits. You could probably cover ground fairly fast."

"Oh man, the plan was to conduct one good interview, not thirty."

"Do I count as a good interview?"

"Can you tell me anything about the Edwards break-in?"

"Sorry," Wendy said.

"This *Little House in the Big Woods* is a hardcover."

"Donate. We probably have a full box now. Thanks, I'll bring it by later."

"I could take it with me," Josh offered.

"It wouldn't be any trouble?"

"I'm already going around town. Just tell me where to go."

"Hand me over your notepad."

Josh handed her his pad and pen from his back pocket. She began scribbling.

"What's that?" he asked.

"Directions to the church. Someone from the sewing circle is supposed to be waiting for drop offs."

He lingered there, watching her draw, wondering what the harm would be in questioning people later. It wasn't the coolness of the garage that made him want to stay.

"I can guess how you feel with all this and maybe how some people are treating you, but Mrs. Edwards is not a bad person. Don't forget that. However you feel, she's the one that's shaken up."

"You're probably right," Josh said.

Wendy flipped to a new page and wrote something else out, "There, that's Mrs. Edwards' address over on Acolapissa Drive. And I made a little sketch of her neck of the woods. I'd say of all the houses you go to, steer clear of that one. You may not get a warm welcome."

"I don't think I'll get a warm welcome from anyone."

"I'm sure someone'll open up to you."

"Easy for you to say. You're a waitress."

"What does that mean?"

"You work with people every day. You, you have a way with people," Josh stammered.

"Everyone has a way with people."

"I don't."

"Maybe you just need to find a new way."

Josh biked back to the main road. The box weighed more than he anticipated and he had to pedal slowly, maneuvering a balance. Bringing the donations to church and only talking to people he happened upon on his way appeared the best plan.

A farmer drove his tractor through rows of wild greens dotted with little white flowers. Thick black chevron-grooved rubber tires covered white wheels. Its body sported a beat up primary blue. Josh had a toy tractor as a child, made of metal, but he couldn't remember exactly what it looked like with the real deal there in front of him.

The tractor headed in his direction, tilling the soil. Josh didn't know how to indicate he'd like to talk and was afraid to interrupt the man's work. He gave a friendly wave which the farmer reciprocated. So Josh took a deep breath, got off his bike and walked to the edge of the field. Within forty feet of him, the farmer let the engine idle. Josh took this as his cue and walked out to meet him. The farmer got down, leaning on the side of the tractor while he waited.

"Didn't mean to interrupt," Josh said.

"I could use a break." The farmer had hard chiseled features and eyes that had seen a thing or two, but were still kind.

"I want…" Josh stopped, quietly repeating it to himself, "I want." Wendy was right. He needed a new tactic. He looked around trying to come up with something and finally blurted out, "What crop are you growing?"

"Crop rotation crop. Legumes. Puts nitrates back in the soil. Next year it'll be soy beans."

"They're putting soy in everything now, baby formula, muffins."

"Good market for soy," the farmer said.

Josh looked out at the rows of ferny leafed legumes.

He'd been focusing on the temperature and heavy humidity and only now realized the air was clean and fresh. The farmer touched a stalk of green before him, letting the leaves pass through his fingers.

"What happened over at the Edwards house?" the farmer asked.

"I'm trying to find out. No one will help me."

The farmer stood quiet, thinking. He took off his mesh backed cap and wiped his forehead with his shirt sleeve.

"It's strange. Trying to make a good home for her two girls. Moved into that bigger place. Had some work done to make it nice for them." A short lived zephyr gave relief from the heat and the farmer closed his eyes to feel it on his face. "Unfortunately, she has a habit of paying her handyman late." Josh perked up. "If at all," the farmer added.

"Who was her handyman?"

"Do you know Clive? Clive Hennessey?"

"We've met," Josh said.

"Maybe he went over to talk and let himself in, made a snack. She could have exaggerated the rest."

"You think she made some stuff up?"

"Something doesn't feel right. Why was nothing taken? Only other person do something like that is that boy Christian, works over at the stables."

"Why Christian?"

"He and his older brother were always getting into trouble. Once his brother left town he simmered down but--"

"--Christian didn't do it."

"Tell you the truth, I don't think we'll ever know who did it. It happened, now it's done. Gotta get back to work." The farmer climbed back up to his seat. Before he started up the engine again he called out to Josh, "Good luck with your detective work." No one had called it that and Josh lit up at the idea.

"Thanks," Josh shouted over the roar of the tractor. He followed the crop lines back toward his bike, pretending to scratch his face to cover his huge grin.

Maybe it was small, but finally, a clue. Mrs. Edwards hadn't paid her handyman. That sort of thing would naturally spark ill will.

One useful interview. Josh had a lead. He was getting somewhere. How could he stop now? He still had to make it to the church for the drop off. He'd only approach people who had made themselves approachable. It wasn't as if he was doing door knocks like the census man.

Two housewives in their yards were polite but had no information. One shirtless man with a graying low ponytail said nothing to Josh's hello. He stood on the upper level of an aluminum ladder pruning back the kudzu reaching for his house from the forest and phone line. When Josh called out a second time only louder the graying ponytailed man stepped down the ladder, walked right through his front door and slammed it shut. Josh took the hint.

Josh rested in the shade off the side of the road trying to get a signal on his phone when he heard tinkering. He left the bike and box of donations and walked to the small house just beyond the shade of the trees. Someone clanked around in the engine of a black Firebird. Large golden wings spread wide on the open hood.

He strolled right up to the car and stopped dead when he saw Clive reach out and grab a wrench from his tool box. For a split second Josh's brain told him this was what he wanted. Clive had worked for Mrs. Edwards, had a falling out with her and so far was his only lead. Josh couldn't figure how to question him and his mind suddenly leapt back to Clive threatening him in the diner on day one. Before his brain could rationalize anything Josh ran and hid behind the back bumper. Clive stood up straight.

"Someone there?" Clive asked.

Squatting down, Josh stared at his pulled reflection in the silver bumper. A second ago he could have approached Clive and started a conversation. Now he was hiding. Sneaking around on someone's property was as good a reason as any to beat a man bloody. And Clive seemed the type who generally didn't need a reason.

That was the last thing he wanted, to go to his first day of school with a bashed in face. No one would see the bruises and think he was tough. They'd take one look at his physique and know he got into a fight and lost.

Josh couldn't see the royal blue three speed from where he crouched. It lay too far down the way. He'd have to make a break for it. He slid his hands off the bumper and shifted his feet around to face the right direction. The quick pivot on the driveway made a gritty sound, enough to catch Clive's attention.

"Damn it. Who's there?" Clive snapped.

Josh whispered to himself, "What am I doing?"

"Ya'll wanna play games, do ya?" Clive said and walked away behind the house.

With Clive out of sight Josh should have run immediately, but he and his legs were overcome with fear. The hesitation cost him. Clive emerged with a tire iron, storming forward to the back of the car. As fast as he could Josh crouch-ran. He barely made it to the front of the car, still hiding low.

Clive stood at the back of the black Firebird, looking

around, wondering if he imagined the noise. Thumping the tire iron against his leg he strolled to one end of the back of the car and scanned the area. Then walked back to the other end of the bumper.

Josh dipped his head down low enough that he saw Clive's boots make the slow pace back and forth. Josh couldn't tell which way he was coming. He'd come around front soon. He'd been working on the engine. Josh panicked. He flung a wrench from the open tool box into the forest of a backyard. When Clive went to see what made the rustle Josh bolted on as tender a foot as he could.

He made it to the road and sprinted with everything he had. He ran until his lungs burnt. His skinny arms picked up the bike, grabbed the box one handed and jogged along with both for a stretch. He threw his leg over the seat and without stopping his momentum, fled.

He put space between him and Clive fast. That was his only lead. It didn't matter. Josh needed to think out his line and tone of questioning before he went back there. An interrogation of Clive Hennessey was not something he wanted to wing, especially while the man felt that comfortable with a tire iron.

He thought he made a clean getaway, but what if Clive figured he'd been duped and hopped in his Firebird to track down whoever was on his property. Josh needed a hideout for a solid ten minutes, if only to catch his breath and think. Not far down he saw it.

In an open two car garage an old man sanded his woodwork. He looked only a few short years away from becoming fully bald. However, what remained of his white strands had been styled with a side part and combed back. He was probably quite dapper in his day. The old man toiled away in the dim light of the deep garage. Daylight streamed in from the open door, stopping in a sharp line at the base of the worktable's legs. Near the doorway Josh spotted a small pile of sawdust where carpenter ants had taken to the wall.

"Young fella, can you get this paint open?" the old man asked. Josh came in and sat on a nearby stool, stuck a screwdriver around the edge of the half gallon can and pried it open, revealing a bright pink. The man finished sanding one of many completed birdhouses that littered his workbench. "Daughter-in-law got me all this to occupy my time. I didn't ask for it," he said dipping his brush in the paint. He seemed to have a lapse of some sort and looked to Josh as if he just appeared. "I didn't see you there, young fella. What's your name? Whatcha doin' here?"

"Uh, my name is Josh. I'm trying to find out about the Edwards break-in." The old man looked confused. "And I, um, opened your paint a minute ago."

"Right, right, pink's supposed to be calming. They paint jail cells pink sometimes, calms the prisoners. Don't know why I care. My life's so calm my mind's turning to mush. Wish I still had my Cadillac." Josh nodded in agreement, ready to go, but not sure how to leave.

"Why don't you have your car anymore?" Josh asked, not really interested in the answer.

"Daughter-in-law sold it! Sold my house out from under me. Sold my life away at a, at a yard sale. But when she sold my Cadillac..." he steamed up just thinking about it.

"So, no guesses in terms of Mrs. Edwards?"

The old man's eyes were wistful, his mind elsewhere, "My Caddy was cream colored, almost butter. Tan leather interior. Impeccably clean, even the cup holders. But if I could get a new Cadillac, I'd want blue, rich navy."

Josh got off his stool, "Yeah, navy's great. No ideas on the whole Edwards break-in?"

"I never know anything that happens. Only people who really know it all is the sewing circle."

Josh suddenly was back on his stool, "Do they?"

"They know everything. They have their ways."

"Where do they meet?"

"My wife, my late wife, Betsy, used to talk to a woman from there and ... hold on, maybe her friend was in the Christmas decorating committee. Shoot, I forget." The old man continued painting his birdhouse, distracted.

"Where does the sewing circle meet?" Josh asked.

"Hmm?"

"Sewing circle? The group that knows everything?"

"Yeah?"

"Where do they meet?"

"Church rectory, most mornings, early. But don't go there."

"Wait, they're supposed to be there for donation drop offs. I almost forgot. I can talk to one of them now."

The old man awakened from his daze to see what was happening and became anxious, "Listen to me. Don't get involved with them." In a hushed tone he warned, "Beware the sewing circle."

Josh felt done with the old man dramatics, "Thanks, it was good talking to you."

"Good talking with you too. I like you, young fella. So, I'll let you in on a little secret." With a frail hand he beckoned Josh closer. Josh leaned in, finally progress. "I hate birds," the old man whispered.

They looked down together at all the birdhouses before him, waiting to be painted.

Not far off, Josh found his destination. The white church walls held several tall, narrow stained glass windows which seemed much newer and more modern than the building itself. No events or people were depicted in the glass, just various triangles in mixed shades of blue, ranging from cobalt to light aqua. Reflected sunlight danced and jumped across the surface of the uneven glass panels as Josh rode up. White roses surrounded the church, in full bloom, and without a dead head or brown leaf in sight. A path of weather beaten bricks and three steps led to the front double doors. Probably out on their mantle or tucked away somewhere every resident in town had a snapshot of an event on those steps. Weddings, holidays, out of town relatives coming in for Sunday service and brunch and they thought they'd capture the time the whole family stood together again.

A brick one story building attached at the back, obviously a newer addition, with a newer brick lane paved to its double doors.

Josh dropped the bike out front in the grass, grabbed the donation box and headed toward the small offshoot of a building. He pulled open one of the heavy wooden doors. Wood paneled walls lined the entryway. A huge painting of blooming white lilies hung on the wall in front of him. To his right, cool air seeped out from a door left ajar. He knocked.

A woman with a deeply ingrained Southern drawl melodiously called out, "Come in."

Walking through the door, Josh was hit by an icy wall of air. The sudden change in temperature after sweating all day gave him a quick shiver.

"Hi, is this where I drop off toys for the fair?" Josh asked.

A colorful play area in the back corner probably entertained the tykes while adults chatted after service. Three long folding tables held boxes of random stuff. Some of it had already been grouped, like the records and kitchenware. The slight woman, probably a little older than Mrs. Tupelo, positioned color cards and fabric swatches on a table where she sat. She wore a big blonde bouffant pulled tight at the sides, without bangs or a single loose hair anywhere. Teased and smooth, she'd swept the whole confection of a hairdo up on the top of her head. She parted her bright bubblegum colored lips before she chose to speak.

"You're that boy."

"Josh."

"Josh," she said with a tinge of disdain.

"What's your name?"

"Most call me Mrs. B."

Mrs. B.'s petal pink pearls reminded him of a candy necklace. A gold sweater chain secured the blush angora bolero draped over her shoulders. The cropped sweater had a soft look as if Mrs. B. took a dip in a cotton candy machine and swirled around. Her center creased slacks sported a hue on par with Pepto-Bismol.

"You're probably the only one wearing a sweater in this weather," Josh said.

"Someone went and broke the knob on the AC. It's stuck on full blast. The church doesn't like the energy bill it racks up, but broken is broken, what can we do?"

"Who broke it?"

"Who knows? You can put the box down unless you want to stand there all day."

Josh placed the box on the table close to her. Mrs. B. stood up to evaluate its contents. Moving the books aside, she pulled at something near the bottom, a *moo* came out and Josh knew she'd opened the barn door.

"Where did you get this?" Mrs. B. asked in an accusatory tone.

"Wendy, cleaning out her garage. I offered to bring it. So, you're just waiting here all day in the freezing cold?"

"Each year for the Summer Fair we ladies of the circle take turns waiting for donations. Regardless of the temperature, we take that role seriously," she said, raising her chin, brimming with pride.

The hostility hovered, palpable. Josh knew it would be stupid to ask about Mrs. Edwards and inched backwards, ready to leave. Mrs. B. took a step forward, not quite done with him yet.

"Why did you drive through such a small town to get to a major city?"

"I got lost."

"Why'd you get a job here? Expecting to stay?"

"I'm not staying."

"What's the inside of Mrs. Tupelo's house like? She keep it well?"

"She does. She actually sews too. You should see her stitching."

"I've seen her stitching," Mrs. B. said lowering her chin. The chill in the room became overwhelming and Josh hugged himself to stop from shaking. "This here's a good town with good people. Nobody's ever locked their door. You can trust your neighbor here. Some people started locking up, getting nervous. Not me. I'm not changing because a psycho is terrorizing the neighborhood. My door stays unlocked." She took another step closer, her dagger eyes fixed on Josh. "But if someone tried to get into my home. Un-announced. Un-invited. Well now, they would be in for a nasty surprise. Do you hear me?"

"I hear you. I can believe it."

"Why do you wear black head to toe? Think you're Johnny Cash?"

"I don't know who Johnny Cash is," Josh said without thinking.

Her eyes grew wide and her mouth opened, taking personal offense. He wanted to ask her why she dressed in head to toe pink. Instead he thought back to Wendy's advice and figured he should try for a re-do, or at least try to turn things in a good direction. Her project arranged on the table grabbed his attention.

"What's all this? Are you an interior designer?" Josh asked.

"That is personal," she said

"You don't have to tell me about it if you don't want. I don't mean any harm. Looks interesting though."

She looked down at pictures ripped out of catalogs, her photographs and different color squares and let out a sigh. The fluff of her pink bolero caught her exhale and fluttered briefly. She softened looking at the photos of her home.

"I'm startin' in the bathroom and movin' on to the living room. My husband has a stressful job. Thought I'd surprise him by redecorating. Make a calm home environment." She pushed a photo of her bathroom across the table for Josh to look at.

"I've never seen a bathroom decorated like a hunting lodge before. Are those antlers above the sink?"

"He shot that buck himself." She touched some of the color squares mindlessly. "I never taken on a project like this before. Feelin' a little overwhelmed."

"I'm no expert and maroon is great, but maybe brighten the place up a little. Take the dead things off the walls. Pick a color you like. Start from there."

"Not sure which color scheme to use," she said.

Josh took a quick glance at her sweater, "You said you wanted to create a calm home environment. Someone told me that, um, sometimes they paint prison cells pink. Has a calming effect on the inmates."

"What do you know about how anything effects inmates?" Her eyes narrowed.

"Nothing, nothing at all. Except for, that's how I heard pink is soothing. But really how can anyone not like that color?"

Mrs. B. put her hand to her chest, clearly impressed and astonished that they were on the same page, "I love pink."

7

The small leaf tufted kudzu vine that poked through
the open window that morning reached long across the
typewriter in Josh's absence. Josh pushed it off to the side
where it drooped between the desk and wall.

Kudzu laced itself around the wire V holding up the
middle of the three framed pictures to his left, the women in
the fresh air hanging laundry on a windy day. Two other
green kudzu shoots climbed just inside the window,
spreading their broad leaves. Heavy rains from the storm
probably oversaturated the soil and gave all the greenery a
major boost.

It was too hot to entertain the notion of closing the
window and without giving it another thought Josh put paper
in the typewriter and turned the platen knob.

```
     The garage appeared to be a
repurposed small stable with two large
slatted doors in front and a single one
in the rear.  Four stalls built for
horses sat empty, the floors scrubbed
```

clean. An old horse drawn carriage retired in the back corner partially covered with a dusty cloth. Its grandeur and wooden spoked wheels now out of style and forgotten.

"I'm off to repair your car, sir," Bert said lining up his tools on the work bench, making sure he had what he needed.

Various instruments of the trade hung on the wall behind the lathy chauffeur. The sturdy work bench stood before Bert, separating him and Detective J. Josh. He contemplated the tools laid side by side in front of him only to replace one to the wall hook and bring another to the bench, thinking and turning. He took needle nose pliers from the wall and put his hand to his chin, studying the pinchers. Detective Josh grew nervous that the repair of his car had not been left in the right hands.

"Repaired many vehicles, have you?" Josh asked.

"Yes sir, I used to work at the mechanic shop in town only a year ago. That's where Mr. Irons hired me from."

"And you feel confident of what needs to be done? What to bring, to use?" Josh asked, still not quite convinced.

"Of course. But some tools have several uses. Others only have one. A plain old mechanic might pack everything. But bringing the least amount of tools to get the most amount of work done, now that's the foresight of a craftsman," Bert said.

"Well, it's good to know you're a man who plans ahead."

"I'll have it right as rain in no time."

"I must ask the staff some perfunctory questions. Since you're leaving, let's start with you." The detective took out a flip pad and small pencil. "Bert, where were you yesterday?"

"My sister's wedding, down near Oxford."

"The day the Iris of India went missing you left town?"

"I know, I missed all the excitement."

"We don't know the time of day the jewel was taken. Who can vouch for your whereabouts?"

"Only my entire family. Didn't know a jewel'd been taken. It may seem a strange coincidence, but that's all it is."

"How did you get to the wedding?"

"Christian drove me to the station. Caught the first train out, last train back."

"Christian, he's the butler?"

"He is. Not a very good driver,

but didn't matter. Mr. Irons went out shooting yesterday. Had no need to be driven anywhere anyway." When Bert saw he had all he needed he placed the tools in a small sack with handles.

"The butler had access to the car all day?"

"I would assume so. If for some reason I can't drive Mr. Irons around Christian's next in line, but it's never come up before."

The fact that Mr. Irons was out all day and a forced entry could not be proven did not bode well for any of the staff.

Bert took off the day of the heist. Did he utilize the wedding trip as a cover to hand the jewel off to someone? Christian had access to a vehicle and with the Big Boss away he could have gone anywhere. And what of the maid, Wendy, removing any fingerprints from the scene of the crime, only noticing the purple gem missing at the end of the day?

Talking with each staff member, then determining who he should dig deeper with was Detective J. Josh's usual method. He moved quickly so as not to allow anyone extra time to smooth out a slapped together story.

Taking stock of all the variables and personalities involved, Josh needed to see if this was a case of quick itchy fingers or a person with a plan.

"Got everything I need. I'm off, unless you have anything else you'd like to ask," Bert said.

The detective posed one last question, "How was the wedding?"

"Good. Bride's dress was out of fashion, but it was our mother's. You know, family things, sentimental value and all."

Detective Josh thanked him in advance for looking after his car and bid him good day.

It was easy to find the butler. When Josh knocked at the front door he answered it. The lights had not been turned on yet. Daybreak offered no illumination to the front hall as the overcast sky absorbed every spot of sunshine. Detective Josh decided to speak with Christian right there as the dimness and quiet made the space seem private enough.

"Christian, what occupied your time after dropping Bert off at the station?"

"Here mostly, and errands."

"Errands?"

"Yes."

"Of what nature?"

Christian looked up trying to recall.

"I don't feel that this is true. Out with it," Detective Josh said.

Christian glanced around, took a

step closer and lowered his voice
confidentially, "I needed a car to visit
a particular lady. She lives quite a
distance from here." Footsteps on the
back staff stairway interrupted him.
Christian waited for it to pass making
sure no one would walk in on their
conversation. "Mr. Irons set out
hunting on the grounds for the day. The
chauffeur day tripped to a wedding. It
was the only time I had access to a car
by myself," the butler said.

"So you drove off the day of the
heist?"

"If I used it as a getaway car I
would've gotten away. Here I am."

"You feel free to do as you like
with your employer's possessions?"

"I'd rather you didn't say
anything. I'd lose my job. I'm still
new here. But even if you did tell, I
have no regrets. How many times does a
butler have the chance to take a lady
out on a joyride?"

A sneeze in the kitchen alerted the
detective to another in the vicinity.

"Christian, are you going anywhere
today?" Josh asked.

"No sir, I'll be here."

"Good."

The detective strode off to the
kitchen. The head maid had come down
from her sickbed to make tea, bundled in
a fluffy pink cardigan which matched the

color of her rubbed raw nose.

Detective Josh feared she'd have no interest in anything except getting back to bed and he'd have to press her for information before she slipped away upstairs. But no, Mrs. B. had no problem relaying all manner of things that went on in the household. Josh had to cut her off repeatedly to steer the interview in a productive direction.

"I'm the only one who does any work around here. Wendy busies herself with socializing more than cleaning. The chauffeur couldn't be bothered to work yesterday. Nobody does their job but me!" the head maid said, followed by a sneeze.

"I'm looking for information that will help solve the crime. That's not what I meant by anything will help. I meant more particular to the crime."

"People getting paid and not doing their jobs is surely a crime."

Finding her draining, Josh rested on one of the stools near the center work table. While he continued interviewing her, he took in the rectangular kitchen. Three doors could lead one in or out. Ahead of him, situated close to each other, were the swinging door to the pantry and a propped open door that led to both the house and servants' stairs. Down behind him, a door led to the backyard. The

glass window squares on the backdoor let
in some added light. To his right,
sprigs and leaves of a potted herb
garden thrived on the window ledge above
the sink. The lightwood elevated table
he leaned his elbow on matched the
lightwood counters. White tiles covered
the walls to head height. White enamel
on the wood burning stove had chipped at
the corners of the oven door revealing
black metal beneath. The cook kept the
space immaculately clean.

Just then the cook, Mrs. Tupelo,
came in from the pantry, arms full of
what she needed to prepare breakfast.
It wasn't difficult to figure out who
she was with her uniform and Josh's
sharp skills of deduction.

Mrs. Tupelo appeared to be in her
mid-sixties. When she walked her knees
revealed the story of a woman who'd done
too much labor on her feet over the
years. She'd pinned and tucked her dark
curls laced with white under her mobcap
with only a couple soft short ringlets
escaping at the nape of her neck.

She spread a thin layer of flour
over the far end of the long lightwood
work table.

"Excuse me, this conversation is
private," Mrs. B. said.

"How is it private with you raising
your voice? Everyone can hear," Mrs.
Tupelo said.

"You can wait outside until we're finished, madam," Mrs. B. added.

"And what do you expect me to tell Mr. Irons when his breakfast isn't ready? Be reasonable. It's a large house. Talk here or talk elsewhere, but I have to start the day," Mrs. Tupelo said cracking eggs into a bowl.

The head maid eyed her with disdain, "This is of the upmost importance--"

Then the last of the household staff, the only one Josh hadn't yet met, entered the kitchen and passed behind the fighting. Wendy, she wore a black dress with white bib apron and tried unsuccessfully to tuck the blonde flyaways back into her bun.

To dodge being dragged into the bickering she avoided meeting anyone's eyes and walked close to the side. The glossy white wall tiles reflected back her black dress and figure, surrounding her with an aura of herself as she moved.

Wendy picked up a large wicker basket and nestled it between her outstretched arm and hip. A little scar above her lip was practically undetectable, but when she stopped to smile and curtsy before slipping out the back door, Josh noticed it. It gave her a unique quality he knew he'd somehow never forget. Wendy shut the door behind her and Detective Josh returned to the chore of conducting interviews.

"I've been sick and I've been restless!" Mrs. B. complained.

"Walking around at all hours? Waking the whole staff? If you're sick, get into bed. If not, get dressed for work. Either way I have to make breakfast."

The quarrel gave Josh a moment to arrange some of the puzzle pieces into place. Yes, both the chauffeur and butler had been out, but Wendy had been here. Here at the mansion cleaning. Cleaning up evidence so nothing could be left to chance, leaving the door to the outside open, removing fingerprints, maybe even removing the Iris of India herself. He had the distinct feeling that his energies were being wasted elsewhere, that Wendy was exactly the girl he was looking for.

An ear splitting shriek from the backyard shook everyone. Josh darted from his stool. He burst through the back door. The scene before him stopped him in his tracks: an evenly gray sky, rows of white sheets, flapping in the gusts echoing the sounds of great sails on the wind, and Wendy, struggling knee deep in the mud.

"Help, my legs!" she called out.

Her basket lay toppled on its side, empty. Luckily, she hadn't stripped any of the laundry before being devoured by the earth. The detective rushed to her aid and then he too began to sink and trudged forward with as much dignity as he could muster.

"The rains turned it from muck to deep muck," she cried. Josh picked Wendy up in his big strong arms. Her legs made a kiss sound as he extricated her free from the mire.

Carrying her to solid ground just a few short paces away he said, "Wendy, you're exactly the girl I've been looking for."

"How is that?" she asked. He set her down near a support rod for the laundry lines. She lifted her black skirt by the hem and peered beneath. "I lost a shoe."

Nobody wants to dig in the mud, but Detective J. Josh was a gentleman. He took off his black suit jacket, handed it to her and rolled up his sleeves. He trudged back, sinking with each new step.

Scrutinizing the gray silty goo with his fingertips, he found himself sunk to both the knees and the elbows. Near his face a sheet corner snapped as it flipped in the wind, mocking him. The detective thought it would be clever to retrieve Wendy's shoe, shake off the excess mud and place it on her foot as if she were a princess in a story. Josh had to remind himself that he had work to do.

"While you're waiting, when did you realize the Iris of India was missing?"

"While I was cleaning the case."

"After you'd removed any potential fingerprints?"

"Yes, after," she hesitantly responded.

"When did you realize you'd left the patio door open?"

"After I realized the stone was missing."

"Again, after."

"Yes, after. I know it must look bad."

"It doesn't look good. I find it peculiar that the one night you left the door unlocked someone snuck in."

"I may have left it unlocked before."

"Before?" he said standing upright.

"It's never made a difference before."

"I see. What were you doing last night?" Josh asked returning to his shoe search.

"Sir, if I may, you can ask me all the questions you like, but you're asking the wrong questions."

"I see. I didn't realize you had done detective work before, Miss Wendy. Perhaps if you find yourself in London you should look me up. We could work as a team."

She said nothing and stood very still. He stopped digging around and straightened up to face her.

"Sarcasm is uncalled for. I apologize," Josh said.

The detective felt cool winds against the wet of his arms. He imagined what he must look like to her, standing there with gray mud evening gloves, and he bent back down to continue reaching.

"What line of questioning do you propose?" Josh asked.

"It's not a line of questioning. It's one question," Wendy said, flipping his jacket over her arm, gently clasping her hands together at her waist, "Why that stone and only that stone?"

"It's the most valuable item in the house by far. It can be concealed and transported with great ease. Someone could have sought out an unscrupulous gem merchant, a lapidary who dabbles in the black market. Maybe the tradesman would break down the Iris of India, shaping and faceting each new sapphire, rendering their origins unrecognizable. I cannot believe there exists a sophisticated market for gemstones this deep in the country. Perhaps as I was making my way north the gem itself was already headed south to London," the detective pondered aloud.

"Oh, you're digging around too deep. It's probably just under the surface," Wendy said. She removed a clothespin from the line and fastened the collar of his jacket by the laundered bedding, up and out of harm's way. She lifted her skirt in a huff and headed out to the ashy muck herself. Down she sank near him until they were the same height, seeing eye to eye. They felt around in the sludge together. Somewhere out of sight Josh heard the distant mooing of cows out to pasture.

"The sapphire is not an oversized painting. There's far more ease in pinching a small item," Josh said.

"You're looking at the opportunity. The staff has opportunity every day. But who had the motivation? Of all the valuables to take, why that gem?"

"Well, I don't know why--"

"--I've got it!" Wendy exclaimed, snagging the heel of her shoe and yanking it out. She made her way back to the kitchen door.

"Miss Wendy."

"Excuse me sir, I have to put on a new frock," she said before curtsying and walking back through the kitchen the way she came.

Josh took hold of the wicker basket by its handle and dragged it to the back door. Looking down at himself he realized before he spoke to anyone else he too had to change.

Josh removed his shoes so as not to track mud into the house. He gave them each a brisk shake before carrying them in one handed. Mrs. B. had since left the kitchen. Thankfully, the cook ran apples under the tap and had her back to him.

Detective Josh made his way to the main stairs undetected. Although a household staff member would be obliged to clean his shoes and suit of mud, he much rather the state of his appearance go unnoticed and that he take care of the problem himself.

Being a detective he was conscious of not leaving a trace of mud, or anything, in his wake. Tiptoeing up the stairs created enough space to prevent his wet pant cuffs from grazing the fine carpeting. He silently climbed the staircase, pausing briefly on the top landing to glance at the grandfather clock. The pendulum swayed in its belly. A sickle moon and stars rose in the arced dial above the face. And then angry whispers floated down the stairs.

"You've been unwell," a young man said in a soft voice.

"Don't tell me I've been unwell," a woman responded in an equally low tone. "That doesn't affect my eyesight. I saw you. Don't you dare tell me no. I know what I saw."

"I'm not a prisoner in my room. Although I'm sure you would love that idea."

"Secrets can be dangerous," she breathed out.

"There is no danger."

The woman hissed, "If you don't tell the detective I will."

"Tell me what?" Detective Josh asked, arriving at the top step and alarming both of them. Christian whipped his head around toward Josh. Mrs. B. tightly wrapped her pink sweater around herself and crossed her arms.

"Detective, I didn't hear you come up the stairs," Christian said.

"I didn't set out to sneak up on you. I had to remove my shoes. Mud."

Both the head maid and butler shifted their gaze down to his shiny muck pant legs and bare socks. Josh too looked down at his silty arms and attire.

"Well, now that that's settled," the detective said, "tell me what?"

A knock at the door jarred Josh out of England and back to Mississippi. He leaned forward to see through the window who would be knocking at this hour. Sheriff Briggs. Josh opened the door and Sheriff didn't say a word. He gave a hard look to Josh and walked away, which Josh took to mean he should follow.

The roads had no streetlights. They drove along without speaking, Josh again in the backseat, the two of them separated by wide metal mesh.

Josh finally broke the silence, "I appreciate the lift to work, but I think the stables are closed Friday nights."

"Watch your mouth, boy," Sheriff said, eyeing him in the rearview. Josh figured maybe he should and they continued wordlessly all the way into the little box of a station.

Sheriff sat at his desk and gestured for Josh to take a seat across from him. After a long unflinching stare Sheriff asked, "What were you doing tonight?"

"Writing, in my room."

"Alone or can anyone vouch for you?"

Josh shook his head.

"Rile the whole town up with questions, then swing by Mrs. Edwards' house on the way back."

"I can honestly tell you out of all the houses I went to I steered clear of hers."

"Now is not the time for your smart mouth. Time to start telling the truth. Right now!"

"What's going on?"

"Someone was just shuffling around her house."

"Did they go in?"

"No, you didn't! If you don't want to confess, that's fine! You're the writer. Write it out. Sign it at the bottom." Sheriff threw a yellow legal pad in front of him. "When she told me someone circled around her house I knew exactly who it was. Already got some good practice running around at Clive Hennessey's place today didn't ya?"

Josh's eyes widened.

"Hurled the man's own wrench into the forest to throw him off? Really, really?"

Josh looked down. He secured his glasses onto face with his whole hand to momentarily hide. As his hand came down he became starkly aware of the bars of the jail cell to his left.

Sheriff Briggs saw a weak moment in Josh and slid the legal pad closer to him.

"Without proof, you can't arrest me," Josh said.

Sheriff leaned back in his chair. A stare down competition ensued.

"You're right. You can go," Sheriff said.

Josh let out a sigh of relief and stood up. He waited for Sheriff to rise so they could proceed to the car.

"It's a long walk. Better get started," Sheriff said.

"Walk all that way at night?"

"I'm not your chauffeur."

"We could have had this same conversation back at my room."

"I know," Sheriff said.

Josh picked up the phone from the cradle on the desk. Sheriff pressed the button to hang it up.

"You got a quarter?" Sheriff asked.

"I'm entitled to one phone call."

"If you're arrested." Sheriff glanced down at the legal pad. "You want a phone call?"

Josh looked over at the jail cell and back to the yellow lined paper. Sheriff Briggs recognized he may buckle and reached out with a pen.

"You went into her home and were only playing around," Sheriff offered. "You were curious, that's why you went through her things. You were tired from travel, so you slept in her bed. That boiling pot, you didn't mean to start a fire. That's it. That's all you have to write. Mrs. Edwards probably won't press charges. I'll give you a stern warning and you can be on your way and in your class come Monday morning, just like you planned." Sheriff gave the pen in his still extended hand a little shake.

All of Josh's thoughts centered on getting out of the station and staying on the right side of those bars.

"Isn't that all that matters? We make Mrs. Edwards happy and you get to go to your class? We can do this the hard way or the easy way. Let's take the easy route."

Josh looked at the pen inches from his reach. He only had to open his hand. There seemed so few options.

Reluctantly, he snatched it and sat in a huff. A smile of self-satisfaction crossed Sheriff Briggs's face as Josh scribbled it out.

"Just sign it at the bottom?" Josh asked.

"Uh huh."

Josh signed his name, tore off the sheet and handed it over. Sheriff eyed the yellow page and his face dropped.

"It's an IOU for 25 cents," Josh said.
Sheriff crumpled it up and threw it out. His usual calm demeanor cracked.

"Make your phone call and get out of my sight!"

8

Josh waited outside surrounded by the clicking of cicadas in the dark. When the pickup truck pulled in he went to the open window.

"I didn't wake you, did I?" Josh said.

"I was up. Just got in," Christian said.

Josh walked around to the passenger door and hopped in. They headed out on dark country roads. The truck's headlights lit the way.

"You were up this late? What were you doing?"

"Thinking about giving it one last chance with Lou Ann."

"The redhead?"

"Gonna talk to her after church on Sunday. Maybe she just needs to warm up to me. We're friends, but why does she only want to be friends? I don't want to nag her though."

"You go to church?"

"Yeah, they serve coffee and muffins after service and my dad's been out of work for, well, about twenty years now. So Mom started taking us back when we were kids."

"Your mom seems like a resourceful woman."

"You don't know the half of it."

"I think you should find a new girl, if you ask me," Josh said.

"Thanks, but I didn't."

"Anyway, someone tried to get into the Edwards house again. Twice someone's gone there. It's someone in town. It has to be," Josh said.

"I should ask Lou Ann if she likes bowling. I can never find a girl who likes bowling."

"He doesn't want to get into just any house, only Mrs. Edwards' house."

"You agree there's no harm in just being friendly after church?"

"Now he's biding his time," Josh looked out the window at the trees flying past. Kudzu had not totally enveloped this area of forest although it had started the creep. "Probably waiting, hanging out in the woods right now."

Christian slammed on the brakes. The pickup fishtailed before skidding to a halt.

"Did you see that?" Christian asked in amazement.

"See what?"

"In the woods." Christian pointed past Josh to the deep, dark woods. Josh turned to him in horror.

"This is so not funny," Josh said. "Keep driving."

Christian whipped out a flashlight from his side door pocket.

"This is our chance to be heroes!" Christian rushed out of the truck, through the bushes and kudzu and into the forest.

"What are you…" Josh looked in his own side

pocket, nothing. He whispered to himself, "Oh man." He got out of the pickup but didn't know what to do. He had no flashlight. There were no streetlights. Christian left the driver's side door wide open with keys in the ignition and the incessant *bong bong bong bong* kept going. From inside the hull of green leaves turned black by night the bright beam shone around. Leaves rustled. A scuffle broke out.

Christian yelled, "Come here you!" Josh snap-turned his head in the direction of the wrestling, to the close knit tangle of brush and vines. Christian must have lost control of his flashlight. The light cast high on the tree tops, shook violently and then went dark. Josh couldn't see the beam anymore.

Josh bolted out to help. Too dark too see he ran toward the sounds of struggle, branches breaking and bodies wrestling.

Someone popped out and Josh let out a scream, "Ahh!"

It was Christian, a terrier mix rested in his arms.

The scrappy little white dog had tan patches. A big caramel spot circled her right eye just like the photo Lou Ann showed them yesterday. Christian rubbed behind her ears to calm her.

"Looks like you got yourself into something sticky, little one," Christian said. He searched the collar for a tag. "What's your name? Pistachio. Pistachio? No wonder you ran away." Christian walked past Josh, who held his heart, still shaken.

In the truck, the dog stood on Christian's lap, front paws on the car door. Too short to stick her head out the window, Pistachio stretched to feel the air on her face. She had unique enough markings that they both felt sure they had the right dog. Something about how small Pistachio was and her wild and free crazy dog hair made her especially adorable.

"She needs a bath. You want to come over?" Christian said.

"It's late. Will your parents mind?"

"They were feeling lucky. So they're off to the Reservation, gambling for a few days."

"Can't believe dog washing is my best option for a Friday night."

"Can't believe this time next week I'll be with Lou Ann."

"Wait, if your dad's out of work why are they gambling?" Josh asked.

"I already told you. They were feelin' lucky."

The truck pulled up to a one story house a couple decades overdue for a paint job. Three rusty cars out front each rested in a different stage of deterioration. The porch doubled as a way station for junk and old broken things. From the back of his cab Christian produced a long swath of thick jute rope and tied the fringed ends to the terrier's collar.

"Here," Christian said. He handed the rope leash to Josh and disappeared around the corner of the house. Josh looked at the rope and then Pistachio. A hose with a hose gun attached lay idle in the grass-dirt patchwork of a lawn. Josh aimed to the side and pulled the trigger to evaluate if the spigot was still turned on. The nozzle sent a strong steam shooting twenty feet.

He called to Christian, "It's okay. Found the hose." He shot the ground one more time for practice. Pistachio cowered as Josh took aim at her. Christian came carrying a dented tin washtub.

"You can't just hose her down. She's little,"

Christian said, and scooped her up one handed.

As they arrived at the front two steps, Christian's kid sister opened the door to greet them. Light from the doorway swept across the junk left on the front porch: a coffee table in need of repair, an old gerbil cage with an empty water feeder, a tricycle, a coatrack and crutches, there on the ready for the next time they were needed.

Inside, the carpeting smelled like they had once owned pets and tried to mask it with that perfumed odor absorbing powder one sprinkles and vacuums away. Josh could still smell both, the pets and the powder.

A toolbox sat open with screwdrivers on the upper tier and clunkier tools in the box. By the indentation on the cedar colored carpeting, Josh guessed the metal chest pretty much stayed there and someone accidentally kicked it three inches to the right recently.

Among the many family pictures on the wall, a wooden plaque hung from a leather lanyard loop. The words had been burnt in: Bless this Mess. Josh's sentiments exactly.

An oval sepia photograph of a cowboy looking fellow with a thick mustache and fringed leather jacket appeared to be the oldest of the lot. In another, two men wearing fatigues held up dead ducks with young kid Christian nearby, covering one eye with a feather, playing around for the camera. Beside that hung a photo that Josh could only guess was his family at church. Everyone dressed up, the boys in ties, dress shirts and blue jeans. Christian looked like a fifth grader, his older brother stood a few inches taller, with their parents standing behind them, a baby in his mother's arms. Down behind them ran several pews, a cast of light in different blues washed over them from the side, probably from a stained glass widow just out of frame.

"Josh, this is my sister, Cora Michelle. Cora Michelle, this is Josh and this here's Pistachio," Christian said. The young girl had a pageboy haircut with straight across bangs snipped a little too short. Her midnight blue nightgown had a space theme: astronaut ducks floating around in silver outfits with rounded glass helmets that accommodated their beaks. She squealed upon seeing the little dog.

In the kitchen the cabinets, above and below, were dark brown. The dull carrot colored counters coordinated with the pattern on the pulled back curtains above the sink. The oilcloth on the circular table had a vintage print of pumpkins. A spoon collection mounted on the wall commemorated all the national parks.

"Josh, can I play with your dog?" Cora Michelle asked.

"She's not mine," Josh said. "She's Lou Ann's."

Cora Michelle's excitement stopped abruptly. She threw an accusatory scowl toward Christian.

"You dognapped her dog? Everyone's right. You are trouble," she said.

"I found her," Christian said. "All the same, hopefully little Pistachio here is my ticket to winning over Lou Ann." He leaned the dented tub in the doorway and put Pistachio on the floor.

"Lou Ann thinks you're cute, but she won't date a smoker," Cora Michelle said. "Their clothes stink. She told me, she already told you, she don't like that you smoke."

"Really? She said I'm cute?" About to put a cigarette in his mouth, Christian instead slipped it behind his ear. "She did say something about the smoking," he said, remembering, "A couple times." He pulled up the collar of his shirt and gave it a whiff.

"Mom wants you to quit too."

"I know. I know, I am."

"I wouldn't date a smoker either. I've got standards."

"You're eight," Christian said. "I've got standards," he repeated to himself incredulously. He placed a mug of water on the floor. While Pistachio lapped it up he opened the fridge and asked, "You think she'll like hotdog or bologna?"

"Hotdog," Cora Michelle answered.

Christian broke off a few pieces of frankfurter and put it on the floor.

"You gotta heat that up first," she said.

"They're precooked. It don't make no difference."

"But Pistachio is a guest."

Before the discussion could continue the hotdog bits were gobbled up and gone. Christian put the tin basin on the kitchen table and turned the tap warm. He used a large serving bowl to transfer water back and forth to the washtub. Cora Michelle tugged the pumpkin tablecloth to get the tub closer to her.

Josh turned around to reach for a mixing bowl on the orange counter to help Christian get water and stopped in his tracks. Along the wall the upper cabinets were open. All the supplies for a large mess sat on the counter: flour, sugar, milk, dessert mix, eggs and a series of bowls.

"What's all this?" Christian asked, noticing it too.

"I was gonna make pudding," Cora Michelle said.

"I can see that. Let me do it. Don't want you burning down the place."

Christian measured out water into a handled pot and lit the stovetop. Josh squirted dish soap in the washtub. To get the suds going, Josh whisked his fingers underwater. Cora Michelle joined in spreading her hands wide, swishing them, until a drift of white bubbles rose, piled high. She gingerly lowered Pistachio into the warm water and they worked up a lather in her fur. Christian read the instructions on the pudding box.

"Is she a dog or a puppy?" Cora Michelle asked.

"I don't know. I think she's just small," Josh said.

"I love dogs with little beards," she said, scratching Pistachio under her wet chin. Cora Michelle made up a song which only had the lyrics of, *mustachio Pistachio*, repeated a few times. The little pooch closed her eyes as they scrubbed her down. After her time out in the wilds she appeared content to receive the spa treatment.

"If I lost a dog this cute I would just cry. I'm tellin' you Lou Ann's gonna be thrilled," Cora Michelle said after she'd finished her song.

Christian took the cigarette pack out of his back pocket and tossed it in the trash. His sister made a disapproving pout, pointed to her own ear and then to him. He grabbed the cigarette tucked away behind his ear and chucked it too.

"Back when we had senior field day they split the boys and girls up into pairs," Christian said, leaning on the door frame. "I hoped to be with Tyler Lynne, but they put me with Lou Ann. I hadn't thought of her either way. First thing she did was lean in close so no one would hear and said, 'I don't care if this is just field day. We're winning!' That made me laugh right off the bat and I said, 'That's the spirit. We gonna do this, let's do it right.' We had to play a wheelbarrow game where the girls held their boys' feet and the fellas had to walk on their hands. It was about fifty yards. I'm not gonna lie. That was tough on my wrists. It didn't matter. Whole way from the word go to the finish line Lou Ann's goin' 'You're doing great! You got this, Christian, keep going, keep going!' When we were done, I looked at my grassy hands, looked to her and thought I sure lucked out getting paired up with this girl."

"Lou Ann's fun. She talks with me and my friends after church sometimes," Cora Michelle added.

Christian reached under the counter and grabbed a metal lid to cover the saucepan on the stove. Just as easy he changed his mind and put the topper back where it came from and raised the heat on the burner. Tiny air bubbles in the water began to rise to the surface.

"You'll have to come up with a better story than this 'found Pistachio in the night' business," Cora Michelle said. "There's no way anyone's gonna believe that. Everyone knows you like Lou Ann."

Christian made a dismissive gesture with his hand and looked to Josh, "I never would have seen that dog if you didn't need me to come get you."

"What a way to get a girl's number, huh?" Josh said.

"And a perfect excuse to call."

"She'll definitely go out with you now. Christian: rescuer of puppies." Christian's smile faded as Josh went on. A realization encroached, crowding out his short lived hope. "Now, you just need to save some orphans from a burning building and you're set," Josh said, still scrubbing the dog, "I'll tag along so they have someone to blame the fire on."

"We're gonna have to do this anonymously," Christian said.

"Wait, what?"

"Cora Michelle, could you rinse Pistachio off in the bathroom?"

His sister picked up the sudsy terrier and carried her off. The little dog's paws dripped a soapy water trail.

Christian lowered his voice so only Josh could hear, "It's not just the smoking. Lou Ann thinks I'm trouble."

"Why?"

"My brother and I used to sometimes get ourselves into stuff, just playing around. We never hurt nobody. We … we probably got on the wrong side of some people in town who didn't think we were so funny." Christian looked down a moment. "It was fun getting away with stuff and, well, not so fun when we didn't. But that's all over. My brother's in Jackson. He's got a job. I've got a job."

"So why does any of that matter now?"

"Lou Ann'll probably think I took Pistachio in the first place, set it up, just to get her attention."

"But you didn't. You found the dog in the woods. I was there. This is your chance to show her you're a good guy."

"Josh, you should know. There's the way things are and the way things seem." Christian appeared deflated, his shoulders and spirits low. He took a cardboard box out of the broom closet and filled it with wadded up paper towel. "Come on, Cora Michelle," he called out.

She raced out, handed Pistachio wrapped in a towel to Josh and dashed off again. Josh pet the little dog's head, feeling sad for Christian. Cora Michelle ran back into the kitchen with a teddy bear wearing navy blues and a jaunty white brimless cap.

"I think Pistachio wants to be a sailor," she said, undressing the bear.

"No, no, no," Christian said.

"Come on," Cora Michelle implored.

"I've got enough stuff to live down. I can't take on

the load of being caught with a mini sailor."

While Cora Michelle pleaded her case, Josh heard the rumble of water boiling on the stove. Since they were heading out he reached over and turned off the fire under the unattended pot.

"How about a ribbon? I have the perfect color," she said.

Pistachio fell fast asleep in the paper towel bedding, a satin pistachio bow tied around her neck. Christian and Josh drove to Lou Ann's without the radio and without speaking.

Once they turned down her long driveway Christian flipped off the headlights. Halfway up, he put the truck in park. They moved with stealth to the path, Christian holding the box. Both boys were far enough back to have a view of the whole property and something about it turned Christian forlorn. He stopped walking and stared at Lou Ann's family house. Josh feared whispers might blow their cover so he didn't ask. Without making a sound he looked on to see what Christian saw.

The grass was green and smelled of being recently mowed. Little flower tufts lined either side of the front path. Taller blossoms flourished in the front flowerbeds and continued around the corners, surrounding the house with a circle of mixed colors. Unlike some other houses Josh had seen, no part of the screened in front porch was utilized for storage. Instead, simple furniture sat arranged to entertain a neighbor or friend who might pop by. It was a small house and there was no way to tell what went on within, but the outside gave an impression the people inside were happy. It gave the impression the people inside cared.

Josh gently opened the creaky door to the screened in

porch. Christian placed the box with sleeping Pistachio, still dolled up in her namesake bow, near the front door. Josh eased shut the screen door after him so that it wouldn't squeak, but at the last inch he let go. *Slam!* Was it enough to wake anyone? The two raced to the truck. Christian threw it in reverse and when they were back on the road he turned on the headlights again.

Josh said quietly, "Goodbye, Pistachio."

And Christian added, "Goodbye, Lou Ann."

"When I heard why you were here, Detective, I went right away to Christian and told him to come forward," Mrs. B. said.

"Come forward with what?" Detective Josh asked, shifting his muddy shoes from his right hand to his left.

Mrs. B. looked to Christian and patted her hairdo, waiting. It did not escape Josh that the head maid supposedly had been sick in bed, but not a single hair lay out of place on her big combed coiffure. The detective looked to Christian wordlessly, waiting for him to explain himself.

"Well?" Mrs. B. prodded. His last chance used up she said proudly, "I saw the butler in the study the night before the sapphire was discovered missing."

"You saw Christian?" Josh asked.

She pulled at her pink sweater crossing the two sides tightly over her chest self-satisfied, "With my own eyes."

Josh turned to Christian to hear his objections, but the butler stood there dumb and looked down at his shirt to make sure all his buttons were buttoned.

Detective Josh did not need to ask if this were true. The answer was clear.

"Thank you, Mrs. B.," Josh said.

"You're welcome."

"Thank you, that will be all," he said more definitively.

"Ah," she said, dipped into a half curtsy and left.

"Why were you in the study at night?" the detective asked.

Christian hesitated.

"Out with it," Detective Josh demanded.

"I didn't mention I snuck into the study because ... I go there from time to time when no one is around," Christian said. "The other night was nothing new."

"Why do you sneak in then?"

Christian opened his mouth but couldn't get the words out and instead led the detective downstairs. Christian stopped and craned his neck around before passing through the entryway.

In the study, they maneuvered behind the desk in the corner with the green hooded lamp. Christian opened the top left drawer. He removed the contents: pencils, a box of pen nibs, a stack of letters tied together with a black band. Once he emptied everything he became very still, listening for footsteps or signs that anyone was near. The detective remained motionless, listening as well. In the stillness Josh heard the pin drop *tick tick* of his own pocket watch. It went in time with his heartbeat which he thought a strange synchronization. He knew Christian heard it too. The butler looked to the detective's chest. An instant later Christian pulled a pen knife from his pocket and flicked open the blade. Josh took a step back, aware that they were alone. The detective knew he could win any round of fisticuffs with his strength, but he had never been in a knife fight, not once. Christian flipped the knife in his hand to point down. With a quick stabbing motion he stuck the knife into the drawer where the base and side met and pried up a false bottom. Still conscious of his volume, Christian placed the thin slab of wood gently on the desk.

Quite a large assortment of French girlie pictures lay before them. The detective could only guess they were French as the women dressed in very frilly undergarments that plainly displayed their bare calves and upper arms. Black lace, white lace and one had cancan themed costumes with the women kicking their legs up high in unison.

"Neither of the two men moved.

"I'm still new here and Mr. Irons wouldn't be very forgiving if ... It will only embarrass him, both of us," the butler stammered out.

"So you make a habit of sneaking in here?" the detective asked, both men's eyes unwavering from the photographs.

"Guess so."

"Was the Iris of India still in the case when you arrived?" Josh asked.

The butler glanced up and around the room trying to figure where the stone would have been and then looked back to the detective.

Christian found himself unable to articulate 'how could anyone care about a stone with such a varied display of photos before him' and responded plainly, "I didn't notice, sir."

The detective nodded, still unmoved from the spot.

"You may want to ask Mrs. Tupelo, the cook," Christian said.

"Why the cook?"

"Don't tell her I saw her. She didn't see me."

"Go on."

"After I left I saw her coming. I hid in the shadows. She didn't turn on any lights. Mrs. Tupelo worked her way

through the darkness using the wall as
support so she could find her way.   Then
she slipped into the study."
        "In the middle of the night?"
        "In the middle of the night,"
Christian repeated.   "I couldn't come
forward or I would also have to explain
what I was doing there at that hour."
        Detective J. Josh needed to find
the cook and had a hunch the kitchen
would be the place to start.

9

The first dusky illuminations of day picked out the details of the forest not far past the open window in front of Josh. It didn't matter that a sleepless night had passed. Like any other Saturday, he could sleep the day away. He didn't have work or plans. Between dog washing, writing all night and a lingering soreness from pitchfork duty, Josh was ready for bed. He lazily rose from the desk and stripped down. After slipping between the sheets he nodded off instantly. As the day grew hotter Josh began sweating and stirred long enough to kick the top sheet off before drifting back away.

Late in the day he rolled out of bed and showered. Not until he tied the towel around his waist and stepped back into his room did he see what had been developing right under his nose. The cute little vine he'd not taken much notice of now appeared rather aggressive. Kudzu reached for the three framed pictures. Full green leaves blocked out all but one of the bluebirds in Aaron's crayoned masterpiece. Green stretched to the woodwork of the door. Green curls looped around the handles of his black duffel bag on the floor and firmly held on to one of the desk legs.

His first impulse was to shut the window but a gentle breeze cut through the stagnant heat and he rest back down back down on the bed, enjoying the coolness on his damp skin. His stomach made little noises while he stared at the ceiling. Where would he go to eat?

It was Saturday. There was a fair. The fair would have food. Josh really didn't want to see the townspeople. He would rather starve in his room. Then he remembered the pie competition. Wendy would be at the fair. He jumped up, ripped open his gym bag and threw on his black pants and black tee shirt, pushing up the long sleeves to his elbows. The great thing about wearing mostly black was you didn't have to waste time pulling together an outfit, everything went.

He took a spin by Johnny's 'Good as New' to check on his car. Johnny said they were still waiting on the delivery of a part. Josh knew better and wasn't even sure why he came.

When Josh reached the fair he walked his borrowed bike beside him. The festivities drew in new people Josh had never seen before, allowing him to wander the fairgrounds with more anonymity than he'd had since arriving.

Big Boss ran the horse rides. With no other rides in sight he appeared to have the corner market. Wooden stands, strung through with rope that sagged between the supports, created a large temporary corral. Big Boss stood by in his too tight clothing supervising, while chocolate mares walked the perimeter of the enclosure. A man in brown leather chaps helped riders on and off and walked beside the horse if a small child sat in the saddle.

Josh strolled past the different jewelry and antique

vendors. All the jewelry looked the same to him, sparkly and thin. The antiques ranged from upscale refurbished furniture and old china patterns to toys and vinyl records.

Plenty games of chance lined the carnival. Whack-a-mole, a basketball hoop where if someone sunk it a sign would flash above 'Swish!' Shooting water into clown mouths looked fun as did the dart board with a wall of little brightly colored balloons. The Strongman Challenge was the only game that had exclusively grown men in line. Each picked the sledgehammer up over his head and swung down full force. Men bigger and stronger than Josh couldn't get the bell at the top to ding. So he felt no desire to try his hand at it.

Goldfish Lagoon had the best setup, an octagon of tranquil Caribbean blue. Curvy painted aqua lines emulated a river's flow. Three tiers of goldfish, each swimming in their own little glass bowl, rose in the middle with kids tossing rings from all eight sides. The center spun slowly on an automated lazy Susan. Gold swimmers in clear water filled bags stayed under the counter and were only brought up when someone won.

The watermelon booth couldn't keep up with demand. The line grew as the farm staff rushed to slice open the thick green rinds. Pink bags of airy confection hung along the opening of the cotton candy stand, but kids seemed to like getting it on a stick so they could watch how the machine worked. The roasted corn on the cob table had a butter dispenser nearby like how they have at the movies, butter on tap. Josh could smell the barbeque run to benefit the Guidance From on High Sunday School long before he saw the sign.

People moved in hurried excitement with all the new amusements, except for one woman. She stood quite still staring at Josh from afar. Two small girls lingered beside her. One of her hands appeared to be wrapped in gauze. All he could read from her expression was nervousness, perhaps bewilderment. Too many people passed between them that he could no longer see and after a moment's pause Josh moved on.

Josh already slept through breakfast and lunch. He needed to eat something, anything. The wait for popcorn was short.

While standing in queue he noticed a sleek silver bullet trailer. The reflection of the line he stood in appeared warped, due to the curve of the body. People before him and behind him sported their seersucker and summer pastels. Josh, in the middle, stuck out in all black.

"Look, Mommy. It's him," a little boy in front of Josh called out, pointing up.

The boy's mother turned around smiling, expecting to see a friend. Instead she saw Josh and her face dropped. She scooped her boy up and hurried away, looking back over her shoulder once to make sure Josh wasn't following.

Then she stopped short, turned around and came back. Josh held his breath. She walked past him to warn another mother in line with two toddlers, standing a few people behind Josh. He angled his head a bit trying to hear, but still stay inconspicuous. The second mother leaned out from the line to see.

He heard her tell her children, "We'll get popcorn later, kids. It's not safe here."

Other people in line overheard and began looking around to see what the commotion stemmed from. Josh sideways stepped out of queue and kept walking, keeping his gaze down. He'd worry about his belly later. Through a gap in the row of food trucks, he lifted his borrowed bike

over a hitch connecting a cart to a vehicle. He wound up
near tables and chairs set up for anyone to eat or relax. Each
table was draped and taped with red and white check plastic
cloths to keep things festive.

Josh rested the bike on a table and looked behind
him to make sure neither of those mothers could see him in
the spaces between the truck line. While twisted around,
Josh felt a hand on his shoulder. He turned to see a beaming
smile he didn't recognize. Finally a friendly face, perhaps a
little too friendly.

"You must be Josh, the boy who ran his car off the
road," said the middle aged woman with pastel blue
eyeshadow.

"Uh, yeah, how are you?" Josh tried to back up but
the chairs posed a barrier he couldn't pass through with the
bike and she blocked any escape route before him.

"I am doing quite well. Thank you so much for
asking. I'm Mrs. Jenkins. I'm sure plenty of people are
giving you the cold shoulder, but I would love to hear all
about-- Whoa, whoa, where are you going? That's right, sit
back down," she said to the old man who rose from the seat
near her. She placed her hands on his shoulder and guided
him down to his folding chair. The old man had a glazed
look in his eyes. Josh hadn't seen him sitting there, but now
recognized him.

"I helped you open a paint can yesterday. Do you
remember me?" Josh asked, but the white haired man stared
straight ahead as if he didn't hear Josh at all.

"My father-in-law. His wife, Betsy, died a year ago
and he hasn't been the same since. When he's not confused,
he's angry. He'll never forgive us for selling that Cadillac.
I'm sure he told you all about it. He doesn't need a car, he
wanders off, likes his long walks, don't you? Don't you?"

she cooed.

Josh couldn't tell if the old man was completely unaware or blocking her out. Either scenario was believable. Unable to maneuver himself and the bike away, cornered in, he scanned the crowd for Wendy while Mrs. Jenkins went on.

"I used to watch him, but I recently got a job so I bought all those lovely birdhouse kits to keep him occupied. He just loves his little projects, don't you? Arts and crafts, don't you?" Mrs. Jenkins said.

That's when Josh realized he was being watched. A few women ran a booth with scattered stuff: clothes, toys, housewares. They chatted amongst themselves. A large quilt with pinwheel stars hung as the backdrop of the adjacent booth with several quilts folded neatly and overlapping on a table. An older, slight woman stood there glaring, tall blonde hair, pink gingham blouse, pink pearls and eyes like talons in Josh. It was Mrs. B.

She made a move around the booth as if she may charge at him. Would she elbow Mrs. Jenkins out of her way or would they team up and pick him to pieces together? If he dropped the bike he could flee, but it was Mrs. Tupelo's son's bike. He couldn't do that.

"Sorry. Gotta go," he said, yanking the bike backwards, knocking chairs over. He turned the bike around and ran. He tried to lose them and get lost in the crowd.

Not watching where he was going, he bumped right into Sheriff Briggs, stepping on his toes. They stood close enough that the brim of his brown hat shaded Josh's face. Josh took a few steps back.

"Hey boy, you keepin' out of trouble?" Sheriff said.
"Trying."
Sheriff stared at him.

"Yes, yes I'm keeping out of trouble," Josh said.

"Good. Keep it that way."

Josh took one step, hesitated to make sure the conversation was over and then took off. Sheriff Briggs followed him with his eyes.

Taps on a microphone sounded over the crowd and Josh followed the flow of traffic to the stage area.

The announcer in a short sleeve dress shirt, cowboy hat and shades did the usual mic checks and finally, after drawing enough of a gathering, said, "Okay let's get started." Josh saw Wendy standing off to the side of the stage. Her friends grabbed at her arms in excitement. "We'd like to thank everyone who took the time to bake such great pies," the man with the mic said. "It wasn't easy picking a winner this year. All of them were so delicious. However, three stood out above the rest. Thank goodness because we only have three ribbons." The crowd gave a lighthearted laugh. "In third place, apple crumble pie, Miss Louisa May Devon. Come on up here, Louisa May!" Everyone clapped for the middle school girl with the long dark hair.

"Want to share any secrets? Baking tips?"

Louisa May covered her face with one hand while she took the purple ribbon with the other.

"That's okay. Someone's feeling shy."

Some people gave a little *aww* because she was so darling up there in her Sunday best.

"Second place for her pecan pie, Miss Wendy Allain. Congratulations. Any advice to share, Miss Wendy?"

Wendy came to the stage in a green gingham check dress with a belt of the same fabric tied in a bow. She wore her blonde hair down except for the long bangs she'd been growing out which she'd swept up to the side and pinned.

"People enjoy sticking to their long held family recipes," Wendy said. "But remember it's your kitchen. It's good to try new things and create new dishes to pass down."

Josh headed to the side of the stage so he could congratulate her. It became nearly impossible to work his way through all the packed together people with the bike. He had to go the long way, around the perimeter of the crowd. He glanced over at the platform. Wendy was beaming when she shook the announcer's hand and received her red ribbon.

The announcer went on to declare Mrs. Beulah Dawson's peach raspberry pie the champ this year. Handing her the blue ribbon he asked if she had anything to share about her secret recipe.

"It wouldn't be a secret recipe if I shared anything, now would it?" Beulah said with a little laugh.

Josh caught a whisper of, "That's the boy, right there," and kept moving, telling himself the gossip might not be about him.

The announcer welcomed everyone to stay for the karaoke competition up next in the junior division. Josh lost sight of Wendy.

"Hi Josh. Havin' fun?" a girl's voice said.

Josh turned around to find the girl with bouncy red hair.

"Lou Ann, how are you?" he said, still looking around trying to find Wendy.

"Are you here with Christian?"

"I haven't seen him."

"Well, if you do, tell him I said hey."

"Hey? That's it?"

"Yeah, you know, hey."

"Okay," Josh said, wondering why he was being

asked to convey such an empty message.

He finally found Wendy heading to the parking lot with a group of girls. It didn't look like he could catch up so he called out her name. Wendy and her friends all looked at him. She must have told them to give her a second because they proceeded to pile into a car while she went to Josh.

"Wendy, leaving already? I was hoping to talk to you," Josh said.

"My friends're giving me a ride home. What'd you want to talk about?"

Her friends had a car and he had a bike. It seemed like she already had plans and he couldn't think of a good reason to hold her back.

"Nothing important."

A gal yelled to Wendy from the driver's seat, "You coming?"

"I'd give you a ride, but you'd have to sit on the handlebars," Josh joked.

Wendy looked to her pals and back to his handlebars then jogged off to her friends.

Josh walked his borrowed bike away and scolded himself under his breath, "Stupid." Why did he say that? He wished he had suave things to say, but he was never good on the fly. He seemed to never have a chance with girls and he didn't know why he--

"--Okay," Wendy said.

"Okay?" Josh jumped a little. He hadn't heard her come up from behind.

"I had to say goodbye to my friends."

"Oh, uh, okay." He leaned the bike towards her so she could hop on the handlebars.

"I'll walk though, thank you," Wendy said as she smoothed out her summery green gingham dress.

He couldn't help but notice at her waist the fabric of the belt had been turned on the diagonal making the little green checks into diamonds instead of squares. Her hair drawn across her forehead brought attention to her pretty brown doe eyes. She looked positively beaming holding her prize ribbon.

"So what's next, state fair? Is there a nationals for pie competitions?" Josh asked.

"I don't think so," Wendy said.

"Maybe. Maybe a magazine or cookbook company is running a contest. They have to get those recipes from somewhere."

"I hadn't thought about that. They do have to get their recipes from somewhere."

"Publication's worth looking into. The diner only seats so many. You can be the one to expand the family business of feeding people."

"Our diner isn't only about feeding people."

"What type of diner are you running here?"

"One that when someone orders the 'usual' I know exactly what they want."

"What about transients, like me?"

"We give a good home cooked meal when you're far from home."

"That you do."

They tossed around different names for Wendy's pie before she submitted it. Josh liked the simple 'Wendy's Pecan Pie' the best, but Wendy leaned toward 'Extra Pecan, Pecan Pie.'

After they left the dirt road and turned onto the elevated blacktop they passed the old abandoned church bundled in kudzu. Green flat leaves jutted out from every inch. Josh felt a little adventure pulling, still curious what the inside looked like.

"Let's check out this old church," he said.

"I don't remember a church ever being here."

"It looks like one. What'd you think it is?" He led to the broken concrete front walk. They stood not far from where the entrance should be and stared straight up, their field of vision filled by the tall leafy spire.

"I hadn't thought about it at all. It's been covered for years and years. I don't remember what's underneath." She turned her gaze down to one of the few shoots of purple florets poking out from the kudzu.

"How many houses have you seen with a tall steeple like that? What else could it be? It's gotta be a church."

"I guess, nothing else is shaped like that," Wendy said still not convinced.

They both yanked at the woody vines which had woven through each other, again and again over time. This kudzu was too old and rigid and established to be pulled apart. It quickly became apparent they weren't going through. Josh grabbed hold of the bottom and pulled up, like a blanket for Wendy to duck under. The vines burdened him like a hefty chainmail curtain. His skinny arms still hurt from the stables. After Wendy, Josh followed underneath. The weight of the dead vines swung down when he let go. It gave a strong swift shove against the closed door, pushing them in a close crush. Josh gave a brief groan in pain.

"We're closer than we were before," he said, trying to stay positive.

Sunlight from within highlighted a gap between the door and the frame. Someone had removed the doorknob and lock, leaving two perfect circular openings. The green ropes grew through the holes and bound the entryway shut. Josh moved Wendy aside protectively. He pushed his back up against the woven woody wall to create room and, taking the opportunity to act out his action star fantasies, kicked the door in.

The dead kudzu stripped enough that they could pass through sideways. Josh no longer felt his foot or ankle and hoped it wouldn't swell to a melon in front of Wendy.

The soft pink of sunset fought through the leaves and dirty windows. No pews. No altar. Just someone's home that nature had taken over long ago.

They had walked into a living room. A couch and two comfy chairs, still set up for a gathering, faced a TV stand with the TV absent. In the back bedroom they found a bedframe stripped of its mattress. The past resident took machinery or a computer with him, but left a tangle of cable cords behind. The kudzu found a kindred spirit in them and wound itself around the white and black wires.

"I remember. I remember now," Wendy said. "No one's lived here since I was real young." She leaned down and grabbed a white cord tugging it from a vine's grip. "He drove the big rigs in his younger years and what he liked best was talking over the radio. He used to tell jokes on the CB. I remember he told my daddy his favorite part was when he'd hear truckers laugh because they couldn't just laugh, they had to press the button on the handheld to let him know they were laughin'. He liked that. Anyhow, when he retired he developed an amateur radio show out of his home and set up the huge antenna on top of his roof. 'The Breaker 1-9 Show,' that's what it was. It got real popular and some station hired him. So he picked up and left for his dream job."

"The transmission antenna, that's what made it look like a steeple. With everything covered in green I couldn't tell," Josh said.

"For a second I thought it was a church too. Hadn't thought about him in forever," Wendy said. Josh peered out a broken window. "One Halloween he put a ball of twine and a nickel in my sack and then we didn't come here trick or treating no more. I was real young but I remember that."

"Twine? Do you think he went crazy?"

"To be honest I think he forgot it was Halloween and tried to make do with what he had."

Something scampered in another room. They looked at each other, horrified, and ran for the door. Getting out required far less effort than getting in.

Josh picked up his borrowed blue bike he'd left lying out front and they made their way to the elevated road.

Cotton grew far and wide on either side. The setting sun streaked the sky magenta. The vibrant light reflected down on the cotton, giving the fields a lovely fruit punch color.

"What have you been writing?" Wendy asked.

"An old-fashioned British mystery."

"Who's the culprit?"

"Don't know yet," Josh said.

"Aren't you the writer?"

"In a manner of speaking. But once you breathe a little life into the characters, set things in motion, sometimes the story takes on a life of its own."

Josh handed the bike handles over to Wendy to hold and side stepped down the incline to the cotton, picking stems for a little bouquet. He lost his balance on the way up and grasped at a roadside plant, steadying himself. A sprig of the frilly fanned out white flower broke off in his hand during the near tumble. He tucked it in the bouquet as if that had been his plan all along, hiked back to the paved road and handed the tufted nosegay to Wendy.

"Cotton and Queen Anne's Lace, you're sweet," Wendy said taking it from him.

In a few minutes, when the sun finally disappeared, the fields and fluff in her hands would be white again, but at that moment everything was rosy.

Josh thought Wendy blushed, but couldn't tell for sure with the lighting.

They made a left onto Song Brook Lane. Josh noticed Wendy kept her eyes on the cotton bundle in her hands instead of looking at him. Did she think his substitute for flowers was lame? Maybe. She couldn't be shy all of a sudden. It made more sense that his usual fears were coming true. They weren't on the same page at all.

"Thanks for walking me home," Wendy said, stopping to face him once they arrived at her house.

"What're you doing now? Night is young," Josh said, hoping.

"I told one of the other waitresses I'd cover the tail end of her shift."

It figured. She had 'plans.' That's how it usually went and Josh didn't believe her.

"Yeah, I bet," he said.

"Maybe I'll see you at church tomorrow."

"Why at church?"

"Everyone goes to church."

Josh shrugged.

"Either way, you're welcome if you change your mind." She lingered for a time biting her lower lip. When Josh didn't say anything else she headed up the walk to her front door.

"Wait, before you go," Josh blurted out. Wendy came back down the path and he wished he had kept his mouth shut. "What do you uh, what do you do with your friends? We could do something like that sometime."

"Sounds like fun. We could do something together. But I don't know that I'm lookin' for a new friend," she said taking a step closer, narrowing the gap between them.

"Yeah, I figured. See you around." And without another word Josh hopped on his bike and pedaled off into the sunset. As usual, he always misread girls, but he surprised himself that he was off base with Wendy. He thought maybe she was interested and maybe he could take her out on a date before he left. At the very least she'd want to be friends, he thought. He'd walked her home. Why did she let him walk her home if she didn't even want to be friends? He'd never thought of her as stuck up.

Before the evening light completely dwindled away Josh pulled off the road to gather his thoughts. He yanked at the kudzu leaves and threw them around, aggravated and not knowing what to do with himself.

"Thought you flew the coop on your bike," Christian said, pulling his truck to a stop.

"How'd you know to find me here?" Josh asked.

"This may shock you, but I wasn't looking for you. Why, are you lost? Praying for a rescue party?"

Josh shook his head.

"Didn't see you at the fair," Christian said.

Josh threw the last twig he had in his hands.

"What're you doing playing in the woods? People'll think you're a psycho."

"Thinking it was a big mistake to have you turn around yesterday," Josh said.

"Tomorrow's Sunday. I'll still take you."

"You will?"

"Said I would, didn't I? Got some stuff I need to take care of during the day. I'll swing by around eight."

"Won't it be a long drive back that late?"

"Nah, no speed traps late at night. I can fly back."

"Still, I should have left as soon as possible. Also, that Wendy is kind of a, I don't know," Josh said.

"I know, she's a real bright light and she's nice."

"She's not that nice," Josh said, looking back the way he came.

"She's nice and pretty."

"Not that pretty. She has that little scar," Josh added, rubbing his upper lip with his forefinger.

"I kinda like that."

"Me too. It's that little something that draws attention to her lips. Makes you want to kiss her, if you liked her."

"You like her?" Christian asked.

"No, she's fun to talk to, but I don't think of her that way."

"I never did either, I guess. But you're right, she's pretty and fun to talk to. I don't know why she doesn't have a fella. You sure you don't like her?"

"Not at all," Josh said.

"I didn't eat at the fair. Too much sugary stuff. Wanna get a bite?"

They pulled up to the diner in Christian's pickup with the borrowed bike in the back.

"You've got to be kidding. Is there nowhere else to eat in this town?" Josh asked.

"You wanna eat somewhere else it's gonna be a drive, and I mean a drive."

Josh looked down at his stomach. He'd gone to the fair to get food, got scared off the popcorn line and still hadn't eaten. His belly began groaning. Christian heard it too.

"That settles it," Christian said, put the truck in park and pocketed the keys.

New faces filled the diner with the fair going on in town. Christian and Josh took the only open booth. Wendy came to their table, her green check fairgrounds dress gone, replaced by the light blue uniform with the white zipper pull in front. She avoided eye contact with Josh. Josh looked down at his hands.

"How ya'll doin'?" Wendy asked.

"I'm doin' fine. How you doin', Wendy?" Christian said.

"Doin' alright. What can I get you?"

"I'll start off with a Coke, but honestly I came down here to tell you I think you're easy to talk to and pretty. I'd like to get to know you better," Christian said.

Josh's eyes widened.

"How about I take you out bowling? I mean whatever you want. I just want to show you a good time," Christian said. Josh was shocked, Wendy flattered.

"Sounds like fun. When you want to get together?" Wendy asked, tucking her hair behind her ears.

"How's tomorrow? Oh, I forgot. Tomorrow night Josh and I have a, a thing. How about Monday? Monday evening good?" Christian asked.

"Looks like you got yourself a date," Wendy said. She turned to Josh. "Can I get you anything?"

Josh looked back down at his hands, "Soda ... for now."

Josh had a slouch in his shoulders as he biked his way back to Mrs. Tupelo's house. His borrowed bike didn't have a clip light and no road here had streetlights. The high forest on either side looked dark and bleak. No moon in sight, the stars offered the only faint hint of his surroundings. Josh stopped pedaling to look up. The intensity of the darkness brought out more stars than he knew the sky had. As he turned his face down from the luminous heavens he realized he couldn't remember the last time he felt so miserable.

After going over the events of the last few hours Josh saw that perhaps Wendy had been flirting with him. Perhaps he gave her the idea *he* wasn't interested. But only perhaps. He probably misread the whole situation. He often misinterpreted things with girls. And maybe, just maybe, he'd let old situations ruin things with Wendy. Maybe he was too busy tripping over his own past to let a good thing happen now.

Through the low swinging branches of the oak tree that took up the whole front yard, Josh saw the kitchen light on. He thought it might be nice to see Mrs. Tupelo if she was still up since he had a hard day.

He went to cover the borrowed bike under the bright blue tarp as usual, but couldn't pick the covering up. It was caught on something. Kudzu worked its way through the grommet holes on the ends, binding it to the ground. After ripping the plastic sheet from the young vines' grip Josh leaned the bike under his desk window and draped the tarp over. He headed to the kitchen around the front. The back path behind the house Mrs. Tupelo created with the clippers only a couple days ago, long grown over.

At the kitchen table Mrs. Tupelo did her needlepoint on Josh's future curtains. The milky glass lamp with yellow eyed daisies hung above her, lighting her work. The radio on the counter played old '50s favorites she'd turned down low. Josh knocked.

"Hello, Josh, have a seat. Are you hungry?"

"I just ate. Wanted to say hi before I went to bed."

"Should I wake you for church tomorrow?" Mrs. Tupelo asked.

"I'm gonna pass, but put in a good word for me. I could use it."

"Suit yourself."

"How's the sewing coming?"

She held it out to show him. Moving from one end to the next she left a swath of neatly finished eyelet flowers in her wake where a series of cut holes had been before.

"Looks great," Josh said.

"It's coming along, coming along. Something not refined about it. Can't quite place it. It's frustrating when you're doing your best, but you're best is just fumbling through. Still not certain what's really working or not."

Josh nodded to himself a little, "I know that feeling. I hate that feeling. It looks great though."

"That's kind of you to say. I have gotten better over the last few months." Mrs. Tupelo looked at a detail of her work up close and shook her head. "I'm going to bring this to Mrs. Keets when I'm done. Try one more time to get into the sewing circle."

"I don't know that you need them."

"I could bumble around clumsy with my needle and thread or I can go where it all happens. If you want all the answers to anything you have to go to the source."

She pulled the needle through and gave a gentle tug on the thread. Josh sat with her and watched things come together one stitch at a time.

He wished her good luck and headed over to his room. Somewhere in the darkness, between the kitchen door and his own, a lightbulb went off for Josh. The source.

That's where the answers would be. His head hit the pillow with that thought in mind and continued as he drifted off, that the answers would all be discovered at the source.

10

Brazen, yes. Stupid, probably. However, with everyone at church in the morning and a guaranteed getaway in the evening it was too good an opportunity to pass up. Thanks to Wendy jotting down the address and her quick sketch map, Josh would be able to find the house easily. After all the efforts he put in to interviewing people, how could he leave town without checking for clues at the source of his troubles?

He waited until he heard Mrs. Tupelo drive off for church. That way he could be sure service would begin soon. He pedaled like a pacesetter all the way to the farther reaches of Acolapissa Drive.

The Edwards house was set back off the road. The street went up an incline and the property continued up a hill. The front yard was a long expanse of grass, probably a hundred yard dash, if it came to that.

Two stories, white, simple and tall, the house looked like the type kids draw, a skinny rectangle with a dark triangle on top. The property lacked any flowerbeds or plants except for a lone evergreen shrub between the house and driveway. The sparseness opened an eerie sensation in Josh. Gray white cloud cover migrated across the sky.

No garage to hide a car and no vehicle parked anywhere. The driveway ran along the left of the house. From there the land sloped down a long grassy hill. Positioned peculiarly, the house sat in the back right of the property. Only thirty feet separated the house from the wall of woods that shot up around the back corner. Like most of the land around town, if it wasn't owned it wasn't cleared.

Josh biked past the Edwards house a few times to make sure it looked empty. He built momentum and coasted up the driveway. The bike gears clicked as he advanced. When gravity took hold and the impetus slowed, Josh got off and walked his borrowed bike beside him. He didn't want to be separated from it in case he had to take off fast.

He did a full two loops circling the house, taking a wide berth the first time and spiraling closer on the second. The morning dew worked its way into the seams of his shoes, and the tips of his toes become damp.

The back porch ran the length of the house from edge to edge. The floorboards, ceiling and steps were a dark green. Four white metal café chairs surrounded a square white table. Little punched holes formed a design in the metal on the tabletop and seats.

Two steps led to the porch. The porch led to a white screen door followed by a glass topped door. Three windows in a row ran to the left of the back entrance. Sheer white curtains covered the bottom half of the windows, the hems folded over six inches deep. If he went up he could probably see in a bit.

The first step let out an aching creak under Josh's foot. He held his other foot suspended, afraid to take the next step. Josh waited to see if he'd alarmed anyone inside. Birds chirped in the woods, the wind hushed out a sigh, but no sounds came from the within Edwards house. Josh shifted his weight to the next step in slow motion. Although the board bowed under him it didn't cause a ruckus. He waited again, gathering courage.

A beveled wood strip separated the two screens set in the door. The white paint had worn down in spots, revealing a gray grain the shade of driftwood. The door pull arced out, black, glossy, smooth.

Someone had put their foot through the bottom screen, or an animal had clawed through. A meticulous hand had taken black thread to try and match the mesh and mimic the hatch weave of the screen, threading it back and forth, in and out. The fixup was only detectable where the two materials met.

Josh moved up one more notch. Finally on the lip of the pine green porch, he saw into the kitchen.

As the only room at the back, the kitchen was large compared to the house as a whole. People probably built the foundation back in a time when most aspects of daily life happened in a kitchen: cooking, canning, laundry, mending.

He stood a mere three paces from the screen door, the black handle buckling out toward him. Above the trio of sheer curtains Josh saw light sage walls, wooden cabinets, a vertical two door fridge. Nothing seemed out of the ordinary. But really, it was hard to see.

Josh crept a step forward. The porch groaned taking his weight. Was it the moisture in the air? Why did everything have to be so loud? Should he take his shoes off? He wanted to move quick, but had to go slow to go quiet.

Straight ahead past the kitchen, through to the dining

room, Josh made out what looked like the side of a china cabinet. He couldn't be sure what it contained at that angle. From the other edge of the dining room doorway peeked the backs of Shaker turned chairs, pushed into a table before them.

He looked down at his white laced black Chuck Taylors. His gaze continued forward at their path to the door. One of the porch floorboards appeared newer than the rest. Maybe a rotten board replaced. The lines of knots and wood rings weren't as prominent and the dark green paint had a sheen of newness. Walking along that narrow strip, Josh inched up quietly.

One last step and there he was, peering into the kitchen. He repositioned his feet under him. What if one of the children had stayed home sick and lay in bed upstairs? There were no guarantees everyone had attended church. If someone popped out and saw him what would he do? This would clearly not be a misunderstanding. He'd walked on their property, crept across the porch and peered into their home. This was him bringing trouble on himself.

But what was the point in going most of the way? Three paces had taken him to the back door, but he'd see more clearly through the glass panel if the screen didn't block his view.

The black handle had no moving parts. The top was shaped like a spade. Three black screws secured it. It curved out and ended in an inverted spade with three screws again. The center bulged, reached out in a way that even the broadest of hands could slide through with ease. It looked to Josh that, in fact, his hand would fit perfectly.

Josh looped two fingers around. His breathing turned to deep full breaths. He pulled. The cylinder spring let out a sharp whinny. A rustling followed.

Did that sound come from outside or inside the house? He couldn't tell. He held his breath. Again he heard it. The woods. Too afraid to turn, he couldn't breathe. Were those footsteps? He spun around and gasped for air as a brown rabbit darted across the yard.

Josh tried to settle himself, his own heart beating like a rabbit's. He shouldered past the open screen door. It leaned on his back, guiding him forward. Practically pressing his nose to the glass, Josh looked in. This was the scene of the crime.

A square table pushed flush to the middle windowpane had three chairs around it that matched the café set outside. The tables seemed twins as they were the same size. But any punch hole designs in the kitchen flat top stayed concealed under a white linen tablecloth.

If someone moved the outside table a few feet to the window the wall would create a mirror image of the two. Maybe they did that sometimes. Created one long table that ran outside and in, having the kids' table on the inside, the adults on the porch, passing the coleslaw through the open window.

White sheer curtains above the sink matched the three on the windows of the porch with the hems folded deep.

The dark cabinets and olive Formica counters started on the left and continued onto the far wall, creating an L shape that ended with a narrow broom closet. Following that slim door sat the refrigerator and then carpeted stairs leading up.

Then the entryway to the dining room. All that doorway revealed were the chairs, hardwood floors and something dark hiding behind the china cabinet. Josh shifted to the left to get a better vantage point. A long, lean black rifle. The wooden stock rested on the floor. The sights pointed to the ceiling. Tucked away, but easily accessible. And again that feeling of not being able to breathe returned.

A hearty shrub blocked light from entering the window on the right wall of the kitchen. The floor with its mustard and olive fleur-de-lis pattern looked clean and well swept.

Josh saw the whole layout, but beyond that he couldn't see anything else. He stood for a long time taking in each item with his eyes, speculating. Nothing presented itself as out of sorts.

Was the door still unlocked? Or had they wised up? Probably not. Josh reached out, but stopped before gripping the doorknob. His fingers lingered around the circumference, repelled by some invisible force.

He looked inside again and then back to his hand, letting it fall limp by his side. Leave the trespassing to the real criminals, he thought, and with that Josh left the porch.

Clues, clues, he wandered the sloping yard searching. He spotted a tab to a soda can, picked it up, evaluated it and tossed it aside. Among other things, he collected a tiny plastic doll with its head missing, a Matchbox car and two Popsicle sticks left behind in the grass. They added up to nothing. Josh threw them in the air to fall where they may so the scene looked natural.

He returned to the bike resting on its side, pulled it upright and walked it where the woods bordered the yard. The morning dew on the grass never dissipated with the sun hiding. The clouds rolled past without a spot of blue. It brought the temperature to a bearable level.

Officially declaring the Edwards house search a failure seemed too upsetting, especially since he'd taken such a risk to come at all. The whole thing was a mess. Fleeing with Christian took care of one problem, how he'd get to class. But once his weeklong intensive was done how would he get to his car, get it fixed, and get back home to Brooklyn?

He could have already been settled in his dorm, meeting other students. Laughing in the quad. But no, he stayed behind, interviewed people, scoped out the area and crossed paths with the law more times than he liked. Nothing came of it. He was still a teenager. What did he think he was, a seasoned investigator? NYPD Brooklyn division? Or better yet, Mississippi CSI? He couldn't say he didn't try.

It didn't matter. None of it mattered. Soon Christian would come to collect him and he would be on his way to learn under one of the best living mystery writers. Maybe then he'd see where he went wrong. Although he doubted his favorite author ever tried to solve any type of crime. He most likely only ever sat at a desk and wrote about it.

Hoping to spot the rabbit hiding, he scanned the yard. His eyes took a long slow pass over the edge of the forest. The lines of the property were clear, a rectangle of grass bordered by the kudzu carpeted woods. A firm separation had to be maintained with pruning. Josh knew if you gave kudzu an inch it took a mile.

He noticed that though bugs still clicked in undulating waves, the birds fell silent. No melodies could be heard, not even a chirp. A cold feeling spread behind his neck and down his spine. Josh became conscious in a stark way of the forest to his back. He heard footsteps on dried leaves. And then they stopped. Someone was there. As he watched the Edwards house, someone watched him from behind. Slowly, he turned. He couldn't see in.

Breathe. Breathe. Josh shoved the vines aside. Birds scattered. He heard the rustle of branches and a quick flutter of wings from within.

Inside, the dense canopy above gave the wood's interior the same amount of light as a basement with one good window. That cold fearful feeling spread to his shoulders and then to every inch of his skin. He became hyperaware that his socks were wet and he hadn't told anyone he trusted where he was going. Whoever was there had stopped moving. Josh eyed everything. The kudzu foliage above had grown so thick that not much green grew down where Josh stood, just tree trunks and bramble and woody vines leading from the floor to the sky. Birds flitted from branch to branch looking down at him, little stirrings from above.

Was there someone there? Maybe the person retreated back into the woods, knowing the chorus of cicadas would mask the sound.

How long did a church service take? How long had he been here? He feared the time to go had already passed.

Lucky no car in the driveway. He rode through the grass until he hit Acolapissa Drive and didn't stop pedaling until he was back outside his room.

He draped the blue tarp over Mrs. Tupelo's son's three speed, making sure it stayed secure. Josh still wouldn't tell Mrs. Tupelo he planned on sneaking out of town with Christian in a few hours in case it put her in situation with Sheriff Briggs. Josh tucked the money he owed her for the room, along with a note thanking her, in an envelope she'd find on his desk. He made the bed and gathered his toothpaste and facial soap from the bathroom. Picked up socks from the floor and put everything in his duffle near the desk so the second Christian arrived he could grab it and go without looking back.

He probably did more harm than good staying. If Josh didn't turn around he would never have misunderstood Wendy and been cold. If there were something he could do to mend that, he would, but that was old news. He wished he hadn't suggested Christian take interest in a new girl. And he really wished he hadn't forgotten to convey Lou Ann's simple 'hey' to Christian. That 'hey' probably didn't mean anything, but Josh had been wrong before. Again, old news.

Christian and Wendy had a date tomorrow night. After one date with Christian who wouldn't want a second? Christian was everything Josh wasn't: clever, strong, handsome. It didn't really matter, Josh told himself. She was just a nice girl.

Josh sat at the desk and pushed the kudzu blocking the open window away to either side. As the leaves parted down the middle it let in some added light and air. There seemed no point in sitting idle while waiting for Christian, so Josh guided a sheet of paper into the typewriter.

"That's preposterous. Me? Steal something?" the cook said, vigorously chopping carrots, only pausing to throw them in a large pot with a slab of meat.

Mrs. Tupelo used the lightwood work table in the center of the kitchen for cutting, without using a board. The detective noticed all the notches across the top from previous work. Josh made himself comfortable on a stool beside her, leaning his elbow on the table.

"I didn't say you stole anything. I inquired if you had snuck into the

study at night," Detective Josh
clarified. When the distinction between
what he asked and what she said set in,
Mrs. Tupelo slowed her dicing to a stop.

The cook went to the cupboard to
look for something. It was a stall
tactic. He knew. She lowered her head
just enough that she couldn't see
anything in the cabinet and lingered
there, thinking, tucking loose curls
under her mobcap. For a moment, the
clouds outside broke up and the emerging
sun made the white kitchen brighter.
She looked to the window above the sink
where the small herb sprigs grew. The
detective waited as Mrs. Tupelo rinsed
off potatoes and brought them still
dripping wet to the elevated table. She
took her teacup and saucer from the
counter by the sink and set it down
beside the vegetables on her work area.

Mrs. Tupelo could stall all she
wanted. There was no way out. He had
her. She took a sip and held the teacup
two handed close to her chest to give
her shaking hands an occupation.

"Can we start by saying you did
enter the study late at night?" the
detective prodded.

The cook took a deep breath and
looked up at Detective Josh pleading,
"You don't understand, sir. All I
wanted was something a little better
than I'd been given."

"I see." The detective nodded. Finally a confession. He opened his notebook and prepared his pencil, giving the point a quick tap on the paper.

"Tell me everything," he said.

"There's some things I just can't afford on my own," Mrs. Tupelo said. He jotted it all down as she spoke. "I know it's wrong to take what isn't yours, but it's not like I killed someone. If no one was getting hurt and, and no one noticed. I mean it's such a little thing really."

"Mrs. Tupelo, little in size does not indicate small in value."

"I know. That is true. I knew it was expensive. That's one of the … well, that why." She took another sip and again held the cup close.

"I see," Detective Josh said, writing it down.

"Cooking sherry can only take you so far. Sometimes you need a nip of the good stuff."

Josh stopped his scribbling, looked at her in disbelief and stood to peer into her cup. He leaned in and took a whiff.

"What is that? Cooking sherry?"

Mrs. Tupelo nodded.

"You were sneaking into the study for the good sherry?"

"Brandy, sir. Well, surely you've had some."

"No," the detective said flatly.

"You should, sir. It's quite good." She raised the cup to her lips again.

Before she sampled another taste he asked, "While you were in the study, did you notice if the Iris of India was still in its case?"

He could already see the answer on her face, that expression that said 'why would I care about trinkets in a cabinet when there was good brandy to be had?'

She said simply, "No sir, I didn't notice." The cook lowered her cup and asked, "Is your hair wet? What happened?"

"The storm, the rains made for mud and Miss Wendy, she, she needed assistance." The detective cleared his throat and pushed his spectacles up the bridge of his nose. "I washed my hands and changed my clothes. Some mud got in my hair as well so I rinsed it in the sink and had to--"

They both heard the front door open and shut. The butler offered to take someone's coat and though the words were inaudible Josh could tell it was the constable, from the slow low baritone of his voice. Josh took leave of the cook who continued her prep work by pouring cooking sherry over the pot roast as well as a spot in her cup.

Mr. Irons greeted Constable Briggs

as Josh approached the front hall.

Briggs turned to Josh and said, "No leads."

"Who have you interviewed?" Detective Josh asked.

"Pardon?"

"So that we may combine our efforts."

Constable Briggs looked to Mr. Irons, "Mind if I have a drink? It's been a long day."

"Certainly, certainly, come right in," Mr. Irons encouraged. The two men entered the study while the detective lingered behind, frustrated, and as the cook pointed out, wet haired.

The constable called to Josh from the study, "What did you find out today?"

Hesitantly Josh responded, "Mr. Irons has good brandy."

"Well, I could have told you that."

Mr. Irons and the constable shared a chuckle. Detective Josh joined them in the study, taking a seat in one of the leather club chairs. New split logs had been arranged in the fireplace with the old ash and charred bits swept out. Mr. Irons worked his way behind the bar, retrieving snifters from beneath.

As irritated as he was with Constable Briggs strolling in and declaring no leads, the detective had none either. He felt sitting in the study with his proprietor a waste of time, but he needed to think out his next move.

"I do appreciate the hard work you're both putting in," Mr. Irons said. "That sapphire has great sentimental value for me."

"Sentimental value?" the detective echoed, remembering something.

"Everyone covets the Iris of India for the wealth it would display. I may be the only one in existence that wants it purely for its sentimental value," Mr. Irons clarified.

Something clicked and Josh rose, "Excuse me." He surprised both the constable and Mr. Irons by leaving with no further explanation.

Outside Josh saw Bert tinkering under the hood of his car.

"Is she ready for a drive?" Josh asked.

"She still has a front light out," Bert said. "Otherwise, she'll get you where you need to go." The chauffeur rubbed the side of the black automobile as one would a horse or beloved retriever and gave it a few good pats.

Knock, knock, knock.

Josh rose from his writing to answer the door. His first thought was Christian had come early to take him to Baton Rouge, but was unsurprised to see Sheriff Briggs, angry as usual.

"Mind if I come in?"

"I don't have anyone in when I'm writing."

Sheriff's voice turned threatening, "Then why don't you step outside."

"There's only one seat, but make yourself at home."

"I'll stand."

"Fine, stand."

"Don't take that tone with me, boy. Mrs. Edwards' house was broken into again," Sheriff said. Josh rolled his eyes. "Funny thing is, seems there were bicycle tracks around her house in the grass." Josh froze. Sheriff added, "Noticed you weren't in church today."

11

The barred cell door emanated a lasting metallic ting after it slammed shut. A haggard looking drunk occupied one bed so Josh took the other, slouching his back against the wall. He couldn't help but smell the other man sweating out his gin.

Not much had changed since he'd visited the sheriff station a few days back, except now his view was striped vertical. A room with a lock could have served the same function. However, the bars, those gray metal bars, sent a particularly convincing message that he was going nowhere.

The line separating the top half in white and the bottom in patina green wrapped around the room at eye level from where he sat. The short blue threads continued their carefree dance on the AC.

Sheriff Briggs stayed at his desk, sorting through paperwork, in his brown and tan uniform, his hat on the desk, his brass star shined. The chair across from him sat empty. He left the air conditioning on for the drunk while he went to pick up Josh, which allowed cool air to build up.

As soothing as climate control should have been, Josh felt sick. His belly had the sensation of sunken stones, weighing him down. His back hurt. Was it the sagging of his spine or the weight of failure? He'd never failed this monumentally before. Probably because he'd never tried so hard before. He wondered why he even bothered. Nothing came of it.

Had he left with Christian when he had the opportunity, he'd be with new friends right now. Along with Josh, they'd all be aspiring writers. They were probably eating pizza and watching old kung fu movies and enjoying themselves. He could picture the laughing, the fun, that feeling of being included. He trusted it was all happening. Just somewhere else, without him. There would probably be a girl there, a writer. Josh would say something funny and she's laugh and then he'd talk about Brooklyn and she'd think he was cool and they'd have everything in common. He was missing out on that. He could visualize the scenario and the girl, but he couldn't quite see her face. Somehow through all the speculation and regret Josh could still see Wendy's face. Those flyaway strands of blonde hair he wanted to reach out and tuck behind her ears for her. That tiny scar above her lips that maybe still hurt and he could kiss it, make it better.

But now when he pictured Wendy's face it smiled up at Christian. Christian smiling down at her. They'd walk hand in hand. All because of him. Josh brought them together. Why did he keep pushing Christian to forget Lou Ann and look for a new girl? Why did he spend all that time walking Wendy home only to turn and walk away?

Josh felt the drunk staring at him. He adjusted his glasses and glanced at the man. The drunk had his eyes fixed on Josh. A low ponytail at the nape of his neck pulled together mostly graying hair. He wore blue jeans, leather lace up boots and a long sleeve white Henley with three open buttons at the neck. On the sleeve Josh could see where soup or vomit had dried and crisped. And then Josh recognized him.

"I saw you the other day getting down from a ladder. I tried to talk to you and you went inside and slammed the door," Josh said.

"I didn't want anyone seeing me consorting with a criminal."

"I'm not a criminal."

"Who else coulda done it?" the drunk said. "You were the only one not at church today. Even I went to church." Josh turned his eyes back down to the floor. "Like looking for trouble, huh? Anybody with a lick a sense woulda left well enough alone, but not you. Heard you been over there three times now. Easy target, she's out there by herself. Got no neighbors to look out for her. Bet when you're released from this cell, mysteriously there'll be another situation at the Edwards house. Unless they transfer you to the county jail."

The county jail? Josh thought being stuck in a small no mark on the map town was the worst case scenario. Trapped behind bars the night he should have been on the road for class, being taunted by a cellmate, wondering if he was going to the county jail all turned out to be a new set of lows he hadn't considered. An ache grew in his chest and in his burdened spine as he slouched farther down against the wall.

"Everyone's got their eye on you. Ya no good," the drunk said. Josh kept his gaze lowered. "You've outlived your cute little Goldilocks nickname. Now you're just 'the psycho'."

"Maybe you could give me some tips on how to be a better criminal," Josh said casually. "What'd you do to get in here?"

Sheriff looked over with mild interest at the comment. Next thing Josh knew the drunk's thick hands grabbed him and threw him up against the wall. The man pressed in on him. He leaned forward with his weight to hold Josh in place. The bed sloppily propped Josh's calves out and his feet hung limply off the floor.

"You and me are gon' be locked in a cage together for days and you wanna mouth off?" the drunk threatened, their noses practically touching. Josh couldn't breathe in the haze of gin.

He slapped at the man's hands and shoved his chest with his skinny arms. The drunk's muscles were rock hard. Young or old, there seemed to be no puny men in Mississippi. The weak ones were probably pummeled to death at birth.

"That's enough of that," Sheriff said.

The man slammed Josh's body into the wall once more before he let go. Josh flopped back down in a sitting position on the unbleached cotton mattress. The joints that attached it to the wall gave a creak. The drunk sat down on his own bed, leaning his back against the wall.

Josh leapt to his feet and gripped the gray bars, "You can't keep me here."

"Where you going?" Sheriff asked.

"I need to make a phone call," Josh said.

"Sure thing. Who ya calling? I'll dial for you." Sheriff readily stood, took the phone from the desk, walked over to the cell and held the receiver off the cradle. The dial tone hum was all Josh heard while Sheriff Briggs waited for him to answer. That unbroken monotonous note filled in the space where all the answers should go.

Maaaaah.

I'm calling Christian.

Maaaaah.

We're sneaking out of town tonight so I can get to my class.

Maaaaah.

"Who do you want me to call?" Sheriff asked again. He moved his hands when he spoke and the curlicue cord connecting the phone and receiver bumped the bars as it swayed.

Even if Josh did call Christian what would he say with Sheriff Briggs standing right there? No matter how coded his words were, any person he called would be on Sheriff's radar. Josh would leave at some point, Christian lived here. Josh didn't want to lasso his friend into his problems more than he already had.

He thought of Christian driving up to his room like they planned for the Sunday escape. Sitting, killing time and finally leaving. The getaway gone. Their friendship over.

Sheriff tired of the wait and hung up the phone. Josh slumped back down on the bed wordlessly.

Class started tomorrow. All Josh had left at his disposal was talking his way out of it, which even he would admit had never worked before.

"We need to have a conversation," Sheriff said, breaking out his keys and selecting the right one. The lock clicked open and Briggs entered the jail cell.

Josh started pleading his case, "Mrs. Edwards didn't pay her handyman. Have you questioned Clive Hennessy--"

"--Shut your trap," Sheriff said to Josh and turned to the drunk. "First, I need to talk to you privately."

"I don't feel like getting up right now," the drunk said. "You can say whatever it is in front of the psycho."

Sheriff grabbed his brown pant legs at the knees and gave them a quick tug before sitting at the other end of the man's pull down bed.

"How long you been married?" Sheriff Briggs asked.

"Almost thirty years now," the drunk said through slurred words.

"We're going on forty, ourselves."

"How is your wife?"

"She's fine, thank you," Sheriff Briggs said and shot Josh a warning look he didn't understand. "In all those thirty years has she made a good home for you?"

"She has."

"How do you think she feels when you ruin that home?"

The drunk put his head down and shook it, ashamed, "She just made me so mad."

"So you go busting up the furniture? That's not the way to handle things when you're angry, and you know it. Now, unless ya'll invite me over for dinner, I don't want to be called back to your house again. I'm saying enough is enough. She might be saying enough is enough right now too. Then you'd really be in trouble."

The drunk nodded his head, still hanging it down low.

Sheriff softened his shoulders and his voice, "I'm not trying to scold you, but I wish I had this talk with Franklin Lee years ago before his wife packed her bags. If you don't treat her right, someone else will. She still turns heads."

The drunk laughed and said, "Don't you go getting any ideas."

Sheriff put his hand on the man's shoulder, "Got someplace to stay tonight?"

"You can take me home."

"No, not tonight."

"My brother's then."

"Head on out to the car. I'll take you."

The drunk stumbled out of the jail cell and the pungent alcohol vapors made Josh's eyes snap shut as a reflex. He left the door to the outside open in his wake. All the AC that had taken hours to build up in the station began draining. Sheriff flipped the drunk's bed up against the wall.

"I guess you're also the local shrink," Josh said.

"I'm the local peacemaker. If I can't make peace with the problem I lock up the problem." Sheriff hovered, looking down at Josh who rested on his bed slouched against the wall. As the cool slipped out, the heavy heat flooded in flowing like water between Josh and his clothes. "It's not just Mrs. Edwards, you and I. Now it's personal."

"Personal?"

"I am always on call. Always. But there's one place I'm not. When I'm there, I'm busy and I'm not to be disturbed." Sheriff steamed up waiting for Josh to fill in the blank. Josh shook his head. "I like my bathroom masculine and dark, deer antlers and all. I done shot that buck myself!"

Josh didn't know what he was talking about.

"You gonna sit there and pretend that you don't know nothing about the pink fluffy monstrosity my bathroom's become?"

And then Josh had a vague memory of a woman ... and a cotton candy sweater ... and a conversation ... about pink.

Sheriff saw the realization dawn on Josh's face and added, "Yeah, yeah."

How was Josh supposed to know Mrs. B. was married to Sheriff Briggs?

"Next time you think of giving decorating advice to my wife, think twice. Pink!" Sheriff stormed out of the cell, and as he turned the key in the lock said, "Maybe I could bring the extra paint and a brush for you here. I hear pink has a calming effect on prisoners."

Josh stood and grabbed hold of the cold gray bars again, calling after Sheriff as he was just about to leave, "You can't keep me locked up forever!"

Sheriff took a moment in the doorway to get back to his controlled self, turned and said, "Know what circumstantial evidence is?"

Josh shook his head.

"Means I can only hold you twenty-four hours. Sleep tight, you've got work tomorrow."

12

Monday. It was already Monday. Sheriff dropped off a miserable looking Josh to work. Briggs waited to watch him walk into the stable before driving off. Over in Baton Rouge the mystery writing intensive started in just a few hours.

Josh had had it. He didn't pay tuition and come all this way to stop and pitch hay an hour and change shy of his destination. He'd walk the rest of the way if he had to. If he got there tomorrow he'd have only missed one day.

Maybe he should run to the 'Good as New' first. By some off chance, if his car was running he could speed there and be in his seat just before the professor started class. No, Johnny would call Sheriff Briggs and he'd find a way to stop him.

Make a break for it. On foot. Even if it took a solid day, two, he could still have the rest of the week. First he'd find Christian, explain he'd spent the night in the sheriff station. He couldn't skip town having Christian think he brushed him off.

He looked in the usual places, but Christian was nowhere to be found. Josh hadn't taken much notice of the big yellow bus with 'Camp Chickasaw' written on the side when he arrived. Maybe Christian was leading a camp group out. Josh ran through the stable to the back door just in time to see the horses heading from the pasture out on the woodland trails. Each horse had a camper in their saddle. Josh didn't get there in time to see who lead the line.

"I'm not paying you to stand around," Big Boss said. Josh startled. He didn't know Big Boss had come into the stable.

"Where's Christian?" he asked.

"Sick. Called out today." Big Boss smoothed his comb over and added, "I figured as much when he wasn't in church."

"Wait, what did you say?"

"Figured he was sick. I think you and Christian were the only two not at church yesterday." Josh stared at him agape. Big Boss slowed his speech to be abundantly clear. "I'm down a man *and* I'm not paying you to stand around. Get to work."

"Would you mind if I use your phone? I need to make one quick call," Josh said.

Cora Michelle picked up on the second ring.

"Hi Cora Michelle, it's Josh. Is Christian there?"

"Josh, guess what, Grandma June's coming to get me today."

"That's great. Do you know where Christian is?"

"He's out."

"Out? Out where? I thought he was sick."

"Christian drove out to the shopping plaza to buy a new shirt. He's got a date with Wendy tonight. Wanted to look sharp. Also now that he's quit smoking he noticed even his clean clothes smell a little like cigarettes. He's not sick. He just called out. But I'm not supposed to tell anyone that. I made a card for Grandma June when she comes so she won't be mad."

"Why's Grandma June mad?"

"She's upset I'm the only one picking up the phone when she calls here. So she said she's comin' to get me. She lives in Hattiesburg, so last time we went to the zoo. I love the zoo. I hope we get to see the tigers again."

"Hmm. The sun's barely up. That shopping plaza Christian drove to, it's open this early in the morning?"

"No, maybe he stopped to get breakfast along the way. Since he got that job he likes eating out a lot. I'm not sure where he is now."

"That's okay. I have an idea."

The Edwards house was set off the road. Josh would have to sneak up. Gears clicking might announce his arrival. He left the bike near the mouth of the driveway and approached by foot, staying on the grass to muffle his steps. He hurried to the back porch, hot with anger. He thought Christian was his friend.

Josh remembered all the noises the green porch made and where. Quickly, quietly, he bypassed all creaky alarms. Skip the first step, ease onto the second. Stick to the newly replaced board to get to the screen door. His previous investigation here produced some useful results after all.

Josh reached for the black handle. He couldn't alert Christian and have him flee out the front. He wouldn't dare risk that. This was now personal. *Steady, steady*. In gradual measures, Josh inched the screen door open, not wanting to tempt the noisy cylinder spring. He even tried to keep his breathing to a whisper. He insinuated his body between the screen and back doors. Then with his hands behind him, he eased closed the screen door in the smallest of increments until it relaxed against his back. He rested his left hand on the doorknob. Pressed between the two doors, he stared through the glass only centimeters from his face, like a kid too close to the TV screen, waiting to see what happened next.

No one in the kitchen. From his vantage point the narrow slice of dining room he saw had no one either. What to do? Without him really thinking on it his hand gently turned the doorknob. The heat of his own breath bounced back at him as he exhaled short pants on the glass. His left hand stopped the rotation. The latch bolt completely free of the side board. All he had to do was push. But was someone there?

The break of day sunlight came through the dining room windows almost horizontally. A shadow roamed over the china cabinet and wall. That was it. Josh rushed the kitchen.

Standing in the center, fists clenched, Josh opened his mouth to call out, but the words stuck in his throat. To his left, ransacked cabinets lay open. Sugar, spices and cereal littered the counter. Stovetop, water boiled, the raging bubbles churning.

It was all happening again, but this time Josh was here. The situation he swore he had no involvement in. The place he said he'd never been. The scene was all set and here he stood—framed.

If Christian was as smart as he seemed the law was already on its way to trap Josh red-handed. Josh's only hope was to contain Christian in the house before he fled.

"Christian, I know you're here!" he shouted.

The scalding pot continued its low growl. On the other side of the wall, Josh heard scraping, heavy dragging. What was that?

"Christian! I know…" Josh's voice suddenly dropped off. His anger drained, replaced by fear. What if this wasn't a setup? What if this had nothing to do with him? What if it had never been arranged to look like a demented person's handiwork? What if that person was simply here, now.

In the other room a shuffling of feet. A longer, more distinct shadow grew on the dining room wall.

"Christian?" Josh eked out in a near whisper, all the fight in him gone. The gray image cast on the wall stretched higher as the figure stepped closer. Josh's mind jumped to the long black rifle he saw last time behind the china cabinet. Did this person find it? Josh couldn't see from his angle. But the answer grew on the wall with the shadow. The outline of a rifle in the person's hands. A strange swagger as he moved. This was not Christian he'd walked in on.

Josh turned to flee. Tripped over his own feet. Hit the floor with a hard thud. He tried to scramble, get up. *Get up!* If the man held a firearm Josh didn't stand a chance and he jerked his head around to see what was coming.

Josh stopped when he saw who stood in the doorway looking down at him.

"You," Josh said, sitting on the floor in disbelief. Neither of them moved as they considered each other. Josh stayed where he fell, slack jawed.

"What are you hollering for? Are you lost, young fella?" the old man said, gripping a broom handle two handed. Josh didn't speak, still in shock. The old man shuffled to the slim broom closet and tucked the sweeper away.

"Wait," Josh said in disbelief.

The old man shuffled back into the dining room and pushed chairs in under the table, creating that harsh scraping wood on wood noise. He absentmindedly neglected to push in the last two.

"What are you doing there?" Josh asked.

"Done sweeping. Gotta push the chairs back. Betsy'll be home soon if you'd like to stay for some dinner." The old man returned to the kitchen and continued removing things from the cabinet and piling them on the counter. "Where would she put the tea?" he asked aloud.

"Wait."

"I swear, I can't seem to find where anything is anymore. Nothing's where it's supposed to be."

"Wait."

"You keep telling me to wait. Life ain't rushing by that fast, young fella."

Josh got up off the floor, "You're that old guy that makes bird houses."

The old man stopped a second, amused, "Must have me confused with someone else. I hate birds." He moved onto the next cabinet, searching. "I'm Mr. Jenkins. A lot of the young folks call me Old Man Jenkins on account of my son is now Mr. Jenkins."

Josh started to put it all together, piece by piece.

"Mrs. Edwards hired Clive to fix up this place when she moved in here. Did she move in recently?" Josh asked.

"Ah, found the tea bags," Old Man Jenkins said, removing the box from the back and turning to Josh with a smile triumphant.

"Your daughter-in-law said you'd been wandering off, long walks, right?"

"My wife must've been spring cleaning, shifted things around." He gestured toward the box of Earl Grey in his hand.

"You were fuming about your Cadillac and your stuff. You said you had everything sold out from under you, including your house. Did you, did you once live here?"

"I don't know what you mean. This is my home." The older gentleman looked down trying hard to collect his thoughts.

"What's the last thing you remember? Before coming here?" Josh asked.

"Uh, let me see … I was walking in the woods. I couldn't remember how I got there and I realized … I wanted to go home ... so I did." Josh stood there quiet, the old man still confused. "So, Betsy'll be here soon enough if you'd like some dinner. In the meantime would you like a cup of tea with me? I already put the pot on." He looked over at the small pot of boiling water on the stove.

"I'd love a cup," Josh said warmly.

Josh got the milk from the fridge. The sugar wasn't hard to find. It was right there on the counter. Old Man Jenkins filled a porcelain tea pot with hot water, plunked a tea bag each into two mugs and joined Josh at the little kitchen table by the window.

And for a time they sat together. Behind them the sunlight passing through the sheer curtains offered a certain white glow. Steam swirled up from both their mugs as they waited for them to cool. Mr. Jenkins pulled back one of the curtains to look at the sky and commented that it was shaping up to be a good day. Josh couldn't help but agree.

13

Josh rushed into the diner. Wendy was chatting with a couple in a booth as they gathered their things to leave, so Josh sat at the red sparkle counter. He strummed his fingers on the counter practically bursting with the news. An older waitress in the same pale blue uniform as Wendy frowned at him and then down at his fingers. He stopped and put both his hands up. She walked on and Josh waited in silence. When Wendy finally came around the counter he sprung up off his stool to tell her everything.

"You're never going to believe who was sneaking into the Edwards house."

"Old Man Jenkins, right?" Wendy said.

He deflated. Who told?

"Sheriff."

"Can't seem to tell you anything you don't already know," Josh said.

"Everything's been squared away?"

"I left in the middle of work to go check it out. Got fired. Had to give a statement at the sheriff station. That took a while. Sheriff drove me to the 'Good as New,' been there the past few hours. Car's ready and my name's been cleared."

"Your car's fixed?"

"Funny thing, they had the part all along, just discovered it today."

"Fancy that. You had a lot going on in a few days here. You heading out?"

"It's been a rough day. I don't feel like driving."

"Didn't you already miss a day of school?"

"Only the first day, but there's no way to change that. I figured I'd stay one more night. If I drive later it'll be dark. I understand deer come out. Driving gets more dangerous."

"You can still get there long before dark."

"Yeah, but class starts at 10 AM. I have plenty of time to get to class if I wake up crazy early."

"If you can go, why wouldn't you leave now?"

"My car's fixed so I can leave whenever. I'd rather start the next day fresh," Josh said. Wendy shrugged.

Josh wanted to say 'maybe we got off on the wrong foot the other night because I was too busy being insecure,' but couldn't get the words out before Wendy said, "Gotta run. Still have to figure out what I'm wearing before Christian picks me up for our date." She untied her white apron and started toward to the back, "If I don't see you, have a safe trip, Josh. I'm just glad everything got resolved."

Detective J. Josh drove up the gravel drive of the mansion and skidded to a halt.

Christian answered the door and

Detective Josh asked, "Where is Mr. Irons?"

"Afternoon tea in the conservatory," the butler replied.

Josh did not wait to be guided there or be presented. He walked off with such purpose Christian was sure he had uncovered something of significance, and followed close behind. The sound of hurried footsteps acted as a magnet alerting the rest of the staff that there was news.

Mr. Irons heard the two coming. He sat upright when Detective Josh walked through the door in anticipation of the recent discovery.

The conservatory created another world separated from the outside gloom. Grand palms reached for the glass ceiling and exotics below flourished so densely they blocked the view of the surrounding countryside.

The arching glass ceilings and walls appeared to be an addition to an original narrower room. Mr. Irons remained seated at a little table in the transition point between the dark original structure and the filtered light. Set on fine white linens, a silver tea service lay before him, buffed to a brilliant shine.

Christian stood to the side of Mr. Irons with his back up against the wall, ready for service if need be.

Without any of the usual niceties or waiting to be offered a seat, the detective began, "I started by interviewing the staff. They had easy access. As it turned out, I began my investigation based on a faulty assumption, that the person who took the Iris of India was motivated by money." Josh put his hands behind his back and took a few steps closer, keeping both Mr. Irons and Christian in his sight. "What if the value was not seen as monetary? What if it had been targeted for a completely different reason?

"Just yesterday, Bert mentioned a wedding dress and spoke on family things and sentimental value. When you brought up the notion again hours ago it hit me. Who holds the deepest of sentimental value in the Iris of India? There is but one person."

"Me, of course."

"Well, excuse me, I misspoke, you sir, of course, and one other."

Mr. Irons shook his head, not following.

"Iris herself," Josh declared. A gasp from the hallway, followed by a shush.

"Iris? The woman in the story is still alive?" Mr. Irons asked, incredulous.

"She is. The lady resides in a home for the infirm and lives quite a drive from here. A family member sold the sapphire out from under her decades ago to your luxury goods broker, Mr. Smithson. She offered several times to buy it back, but Mr. Smithson made it clear that you had no intentions of selling it. Not to anyone."

"I had no idea," Mr. Irons said, aghast at the news, and threw his napkin down on the table in disgust.

"She is old and ill. Someone brought her the Iris of India with hopes that it might raise her spirits and restore her health. She would not name this person. She gave the gem to me freely with one request: that I ask of you, Mr. Irons, for the investigation to go no further."

The detective reached into his pocket and pulled something out he kept concealed in his hand.

"She claimed the heist was her idea, but my contention is she's protecting someone, a loved one, most likely a family member."

"Probably," Mr. Irons said.

"Iris has four children and ten grandchildren. Some of her grandchildren are young adults at this point. They may be a good place to start. However, based on her request and the fact that the sapphire has been restored to you..." Detective Josh placed a bunched handkerchief on the table in front of Mr. Irons. "…I wanted to see if I should pursue the matter."

Mr. Irons took the handkerchief in his hand. His eyes studied the design on the corner. Purple blossoms encircled an embroidered 'I', which had an unevenness to it. It was not the stitching of a seamstress. It appeared more likely the needlework of an amateur, but an amateur who cared and probably did their best. Mr. Irons pulled back the edges to find the spectacular sapphire, an iris on the front facet, etched in so many years ago.

Motionless, everyone held their breath to hear what Mr. Irons would say, even those eavesdropping in the hallway. The detective felt he had perhaps put his employer in a bad position.

"Mr. Irons, sir, regardless of what Iris wants I am still employed by you. It would be of no difficulty to find these family members of hers, if not where they live, then where they work. I've actually already discovered where one of her grandsons is employed."

A strange look crossed Mr. Irons' face.

"Sir, are you livid or elated? I simply cannot tell," Detective Josh said. Everyone waited in expectant silence for Mr. Irons to gather his words.

"The tale surrounding this gem has been my most favorite for my entire life," Mr. Irons said. "By owning the sapphire I hoped to possess a piece of something grand. I thought the story had ended, but now after all these years it continues and I may play a part. I'd be much happier knowing the sapphire rest in the hands of the person it was meant for all along. I will bring this to Iris, personally, myself, restore it to her. Present it as a gift."

"I will give Bert the address for you, if you like."

"It'll be the second time she received it as a gift and this time may actually be more surprising than the first."

"To be clear, do you want me to reveal the culprit or let the matter go?" Detective J. Josh asked.

"I can't restore the gem to Iris only to then throw a loved one of hers behind bars. No, stop the investigation altogether." Mr. Irons looked from the purple stone up to the detective. "I hate to admit this, but for a moment, with her cleaning the fingerprints, for a time, I believed the culprit might be Wendy."

"No sir, in the end, Wendy was only guilty of being charming."

"I'll ring the Constable immediately to call off his search."

The detective caught himself before rolling his eyes. Mr. Irons left the room to prepare for travel.

"How kind of Mr. Irons to stop the investigation," Christian remarked.

"Like I said, it wouldn't have been difficult to continue. I already discovered where one of her grandsons works," Josh said with an edge in his voice. "Borrowed the car to visit a 'particular lady,' was it?"

The butler opened his mouth, but hesitated, not sure if he should speak and ruin his fortuitous outcome, "I know what you must think, but I love my grandmother quite dearly."

"Love, I see, love made you do something you would never normally do."

"If you loved someone that much it might surprise you what you could find in yourself to do," Christian said softly. Josh gave him a long piercing stare before leaving the conservatory.

Detective Josh found Mrs. Tupelo and Wendy just around the corner. When discovered, Mrs. Tupelo acted as if she was en route to somewhere important.

"Oh hello Detective, pleasant day isn't it?" Mrs. Tupelo said and left for the kitchen.

Wendy stood there caught, making no pretenses. She'd changed from her muddy frock into an identical uniform of a black dress with white apron. At the

waist of her apron she'd tucked a
dusting rag. Wendy looked up at him
with her big brown doe eyes and smiled.
When she did, he couldn't explain why,
but Josh again became aware that his
pocket watch and heart beat in time.

"Miss Wendy, your advice helped me
solve the mystery. I take back my
apology from earlier. If you find
yourself in London, please come call on
me. I do think we would make a good
team." He handed her a calling card
which she took with both hands. It
read: Detective J. Josh, Solver of
Mysteries.

"Thank you, but I don't know that
I'll find myself in London anytime soon.
I've never traveled to a big city."

"Don't let London scare you. I
think you'd take to it. And your
temperament makes you well suited for
the job."

"Are you offering me a job?"

"Of course."

"Thank you, but I already have
one." She laughed a little to herself.
"I have thought about it though. I'd
love to go to new places, see new
things. Oh, but don't listen to me. I
mean really, a big city like London? I
wouldn't know what to do with myself
once I got there."

"Let me take care of that. There's
a proper inn across the street from me.

I can arrange for you to stay there as long as you like. As for the city there are more diversions than you can imagine. I'll see to it that it's worth your while."

A wry smile crossed her face, "Detective, you were called here to recover something stolen. I dare say, are you now trying to steal me away?"

"I am not a bold person." He took off his wire rim spectacles to clean them with a pocket square and continued speaking more meekly than he had intended. "However, I find I cannot help myself but try." The sounds of footsteps had them step around the corner for privacy. "Miss Wendy, with my sharp skills of observation and your knowledge of human nature we could solve any mystery that came our way. As preposterous as it may sound," Detective Josh replaced the spectacles to his face and straightened his shoulders, "if we were to team up, I see great adventures before us."

"I'm glad I was able to help with your mystery. Your offer sounds so exciting. If I am to be honest though, this, this life is all I know. I've never even stepped outside the county. Have a safe trip back, Detective. I'm afraid this is goodbye," she said before she curtsied and left.

Josh didn't want Wendy to leave,

but she had work to do and his work was done.

The detective went to the garage where he found Bert cleaning the grill of Mr. Irons' automobile with a small brush and a bucket of soapy water.

"How'd your car run?" Bert asked.

"Very smooth. Thank you. My front left headlight is still out. Would you be able to fix that now?"

"Now? I don't have the bulb. But you can get to London long before dark and the weather's fine."

"I need the light fixed before I return to London."

"I've no problem going into town to see if the shop has one and repairing it, sir. But any shop in London would have a bulb already on hand. I only thought you'd be in a hurry to get going."

"I am," Detective Josh said, and walked off.

Hitting a snag in the story, Josh stopped dead. The actions of the detective no longer made any good sense. Josh took his hands from the typewriter and placed them on the edges of the desk, thinking.

It's fine to go with the flow when the flowing is good. However, the tale's momentum had stalled. Josh had been seeing where events took him. Now he needed to make a decision and steer the story where it should go.

His fingers inched back into position on the black keys of the Smith Corona, but they just rest there. How was the story going to end?

He leaned back in his chair on its rear two legs and stretched. The wide floor boards sighed under the shift in pressure. Tilted back, he gained a broader view.

Kudzu had made itself at home. The wall in front of him was covered in a lush green mat. Other vines needed support, sturdy trellises. Kudzu wasn't as delicate as all that. It made bold moves. It worked with what was already there.

Its greenery extended above the door onto the adjacent wall. Once the vine hit the ceiling it felt no restraint. The green continued to grow, aiming to loop around the base of the overhead light globe. Josh wondered if it could make it. What looked like a waterfall of leaves consumed the far end of his desk, connecting it to the windowsill.

Flowers seemed an afterthought for kudzu as all energies were spent on aggressive expanse. Still three purple inflorescences sprouted up. Down to his right, purple flowers sprung from where the kudzu wrapped itself around the straps of his black duffle bag, even giving the handles a little lift.

Just above the middle frame, of ladies hanging their wash on a windy day, a trail of buds jutted out from the connecting wire V, the lowest blossoms just opening. Their purple pouts revealing a center dot of bright yellow.

Green swirled around the empty curtain rod above. From it a tight floral cluster leaned down, knowing where the light came from and reaching for it.

A slight scent lingered in the heavy heat, a subtle fragrance he couldn't quite name, but something akin to a girl's freshly shampooed hair.

The mystery was solved, his vehicle fixed. Why

didn't the detective hop in his car and go? What could be motivating him to stay?

Josh wondered aloud, "Why doesn't he just leave?"

A flash in his mind of Wendy the maid made him think of Wendy the waitress. And he realized all his questions had one answer. All the things that didn't make any sense suddenly became clear.

"He's in love."

Josh checked the time. It was late, real late, but maybe Wendy was up. Maybe she'd returned from her date. He looked at the car keys on his desk. His boxy black four door's cooling and heating system had been broken since he bought it. Even with the windows open an enclosed area would not have much circulation. For once he wanted to arrive not a sweaty mess.

He hopped on the royal blue three speed and rode off in the direction of Song Brook Lane. A headiness of scents rose from the earth. Greenery and flowers and even a whiff of the newly turned soil itself lingered in the night air. Moonlight reflected off the vast expanses of cotton, giving the fields a gentle blue glow.

Past the crops and further still from where the lemonade stand had once been, Josh stopped in front of the house wrapped in white aluminum siding. A faint light shone through the slim windows on either side of the front door. Josh took a deep breath, walked up the path, thought on knocking far longer than he should have and finally brought himself to knock. The light grew brighter as if an internal door had opened. He heard movement and then there she was. Wendy wore a peach colored dress. One wide flowy ruffle wrapped around the top. It swished a little when she opened the door. A barrette held blonde tresses across her forehead in a soft diagonal, framing her eyes beautifully. Wendy leaned on the entryway with her shoulder.

"Oh, Josh, I thought you were my dad," she said.

"He's out?"

"I expect him soon. What're you doing here this late?"

"I need to talk to you."

"If my daddy catches you here while he's out, he'll kill ya."

"That's okay. I just had something to say."

Wendy looked at him, waiting for him to go on.

He struggled to formulate his words, "Wait, let me think a sec." Josh acting odd in front of Wendy was nothing new, but she got the impression he had something pressing to say and stepped aside to let him in. "What about your dad?"

"Up to you. It's not me that'll get a thrashing," she said with a shrug.

Josh stepped in and Wendy shut the door behind him. From somewhere inside the house a warm dim light washed over her right side. Moonlight from the windows beside the door gently grazed her left cheek and hair. He could still hear the cicadas outside with their waves of clicking.

"What's going on?" Wendy asked.

"Well, I wanted to, uh, how was your date tonight?"

"Fine, thank you," she said without elaborating further.

"Do you like Christian?"

"Don't see why that's any of your business."

"Did you kiss him?"

"Don't see why that's any of your business neither."

"Is that what you wore? Because you look really

192

pretty," Josh said, feeling sorry for himself.

Wendy crossed her arms, "If you're that interested in my love life maybe you should have asked me out instead of sitting on the sidelines."

"You're right. You're completely right," Josh said. "I was going to ask you out when I walked you home."

"Why didn't you? Why were you mean to me?"

"I didn't intend to be. I'm so sorry. I figured you were going to give me the brush off anyway."

"What? Why?"

"Maybe I've gotten rejected a couple times by other girls so I thought it was already going to happen long before I heard it."

"That's not fair. Whatever happened before, you can't take that out on me. How can you expect anyone to give you a chance if you don't give them a chance?" she said more hurt than angry.

"You're right. It didn't have to go that way. That was my fault. I started thinking of how things would go wrong and then I made it all go bad. The thing, the thing that eats at me is..." Josh looked down at his feet. He had planned on this being romantic. Instead it had become really, really awkward. And somehow he still knew he'd rather be here in an excruciatingly uncomfortable conversation with Wendy than back at his room alone. Maybe that's what real romance was, being willing to show up after all was lost and still try. "The thing that eats at me is that I pushed myself to come back into town. I found the courage to ask questions of strangers, but when it came to you, when it came to asking you out on a date, it's not that you turned me down. It's that I never actually bothered to ask."

"Josh, why are you saying this now? Why did you

come here?" she said in a near whisper, a sadness in her voice. It seemed all he was doing was upsetting her. He hated to see her unhappy and wanted so badly to take her in his arms. This was his chance to change things.

"I wanted to say that I misunderstood you the other day when I walked you home."

"You came to say you misunderstood me?"

"Wait. Also I was maybe rude and laughed at you when I first met you. I thought I was being funny, but I'm not funny." He pushed his glasses up more securely on his face. Wendy stared at him, not clear what was going on. "That's basically it," he added.

"That's it? You came all this way in the middle of the night to tell me you're not funny?"

"I'm leaving, so I guess it doesn't matter, but, do you like Christian?"

"I like Christian. Christian and I had a great time. But there was no ... sparks. You came here to ask me about my date?"

Josh still couldn't find his words and fumbled around in his head for what to say, "I came to tell you I've been thinking about you a lot lately. So much, in fact, that I put some of your characteristics into a girl in my story."

"Oh yeah?"

"Yeah, the maid in my story is really intelligent and savvy and she has a little scar above her lip, same as you."

"You're right, you're not funny." She reached for the door to show him out.

"Wait, wait. No, see, the little scar is her only flaw because everything about her is perfect. In fact, that line above her lip is perfect too. It's one of a bunch of unique little somethings that makes her, her. And the detective of the story has completely fallen for this girl. He just can't figure out how to say it." Wendy stopped with her hand on the doorknob and looked to him to go on. "He's got questioning people down because he's a detective. And he's got a good handle on being a smart mouth to authority, but when it comes to just talking to people he's not always so good at it. Most especially with a girl he thinks the world of."

"He thinks the world of her?" Wendy asked.

"Yeah, just took him a while to figure it out."

Wendy let her fingers slip off the doorknob and used that hand to smooth out the skirt of her peach flowy dress.

Josh went on, "There's a part where the detective has to go all over town interviewing people. It just seems way too hard. But the girl, she gives him a pep talk and makes it seem doable. She's pretty great and sometimes after he talks with her he feels like he can be great too."

Wendy opened her mouth to say something and stopped herself, instead smiling and biting her lower lip.

Josh's heart sank. This was probably the point where he would screw everything up. He so often did. He'd come this far though. If he wanted to turn back he should have done it long before he knocked on her front door. The hardest part was her thin little scar was so distracting. It acted like a beacon, constantly drawing his eyes to Wendy's lips.

"The problem is, whenever he opens his mouth, stupid stuff dribbles out. So he's decided not to really talk with her. So he won't say anything stupid."

"How's she ever supposed to know he likes her if he doesn't tell her?" Wendy asked.

If Josh knew the answer to that he wouldn't be in this mess. He still didn't know exactly what to say and figured maybe he shouldn't say anything at all. Outside the clacking of cicadas rose and fell and Josh took a deep breath, leaned in and kissed Wendy.

Her lips were warm and Josh felt his heart flood as she slipped her arms around his neck and held him close. The world seemed to stop and every one of his troubles, in an instant, seemed worth it because of this moment. Maybe tomorrow all would fade back to the way it was before, but right now everything felt rosy.

Wendy pulled back from the kiss, her arms still circled around him. Josh felt her fingers lace together behind the back of his neck. He kept his hands at her waist, looking down into her big brown eyes.

"I'm glad you came to say goodbye before you left," Wendy said.

"You have a strange effect on me. I've never met anyone like you."

"I could say the same, Josh."

"Really? Like how?"

She laughed a little, "You're smart, but a little oversensitive. You're a writer who just started writing. Your glasses remind me of an old beatnik or something. No, I can honestly say I've never met anyone quite like you."

"Well, you've never been to Brooklyn."

"You thought that kudzu covered house with the antennae was an old church and we investigated. We solved a little mystery together."

"We did. I didn't think of it that way. Yeah, we make a good team."

Wendy closed her eyes, raised herself on her toes and pressed her lips to Josh's. His fingers slid from her waist to the small of her back. His hands fit so nicely tucked in her soft curve. Being close to Wendy, standing there wrapped in her tender embrace, turned out to be more wonderful, more perfect than he'd imagined.

Wendy took a step back, not letting go, "I know you have to leave tomorrow, but I so wish you didn't have to."

For a second Josh almost forgot. His class was the entire reason for driving down South in the first place. Everything that happened in the last few days was an unexpected detour. Josh couldn't go off to Baton Rouge without telling her and he found the courage to lean down and whisper in her ear.

"Wendy, I think I'm in lo--"

A car pulled up. The headlights flooded in through the glass on either side of the door as the vehicle turned into the driveway.

"Oh, my daddy's gon' kill you. Quick, out the back!" Wendy warned.

Josh didn't need to be told twice. Out he flew from the back door. He bolted through the wall of kudzu. Grasping and pulling, he clawed his way in. Younger vines tore away but the older woody ones bound together like hardened ropes. Those he pushed and twisted his body to get around. Kudzu owned this section of forest. Once within, darkness.

Thickets and trees practically grew on top of each other forcing Josh to blindly forge his own path. Stumbling in the dark, he held his hands out in front of him to protect his face. Plowing forward as best he could, getting whipped by branches, bumping into things and at one point even having to crawl under. Josh couldn't find a way around a fallen log and wriggled through the space between it and the ground. After picking himself up and dusting the dirt off his clothes and palms Josh recognized he had put a great deal of distance between himself and Wendy's dad. However, he was deep in the woods in the dead of night.

A gap in the kudzu and old growth trees gave a small window overhead that let in some moonlight. He stood in the sparse light, looking around, lost, but no longer in complete darkness.

He spotted a thatch of vines that drooped and bent. He eased himself onto it and the knit portion supported him like a hammock. Looking up at the small bit of sky, he used his feet, still grounded, to help him sway.

Kudzu wrapped the forest in a blanket. A wool blanket, it seemed, creating the largest, hottest sauna Josh had ever known. He stopped running a while back but his body wasn't done sweating about it. Josh actually didn't even care. Wendy had kissed him. In his reclined position, his eyes focused on the small opening to the stars.

Suddenly, his rear broke through, hitting the ground, his shoulders and knees nearly touching. A struggle led to his left shoulder and then arm falling through. With one hand on the ground and his feet in the air, he tried to push up one handed. That was useless. Strung up cheek to thigh he rethought his decision to sit in the swinging vine seat.

That's when he heard the low growl. A trilling of the voice deep in the creature's throat painted a picture of sharp teeth. The noises multiplied. There wasn't just one. Various padded feet dragged through dried leaves on the forest floor. He heard the animals advancing, fighting among themselves, a barking cry, a yelp. Frightened stiff, Josh held his breath with no idea on how he could defend himself. The hostilities grew louder, surrounding him. Then the quarreling all began to move up.

Josh slid further down his vine snare, jostling the leaves. In an instant all animals fell silent and the night again returned to the crickets and cicadas. In his patch of moonlight Josh could be seen, but his eyes couldn't adjust to look out into the darkness. From the pitch blackness, he inferred up in the trees although it appeared they were floating, eyes fell on Josh. A collective gaze circled him from above. When one blinked it became invisible.

Realizing he was of no consequence, they continues their upward climb. Josh thought he caught the flip of a ringed tail, but couldn't be sure.

Tangled up with his knees elevated above his neck, he scrambled to get out of his bindings and flee. With a lot of effort and a little traction he broke free and took off. Pushing forward again in hurried steps through the endless woods.

Josh hurtled forward into a clearing and found himself standing in some type of homemade setup beneath the kudzu.

A sturdy stick held up the vines like a center support in a tent. Lanterns lit the work area, two hung overhead with a third placed on the table. They looked like the sort used for camping, with the loop handles on top and a single crisscross of metal over the clear bellies. The lamps offered a dim warm luminance that brushed anything smooth in a subdued gleam, especially all the glass bottles.

A wily white bearded man poured hooch from a large earthenware jug. A woman with white unbound hair, which grew down past her waist, wore a simple country dress with lace at the collar. She corked the small flat bottles.

Wooden crates, filled with glass flasks, rest on their work station and on the bare dirt ground. It appeared each bottle got wrapped around the body in newspaper and placed in a crate. Probably to protect the glass from clinking together. The glass necks stuck out from the newsprint to show patrons they were full.

When Josh barged through both the man and woman stopped. Josh too remained motionless.

The white bearded man gave him a stern look and said, "Son, I don't know who went and told you about our spot, but I don't sell to young people. I don't."

"I didn't, uh, I was only," Josh fled from the moonshine operation, darting back into the kudzu. He kept going and pushing. The vines and brush and branches tried to hold him back. He fought his way through, finally finding another clearing.

Josh stood on the side of a dirt lane. If he recognized the bend in the road and a bald patch of earth correctly, then Mrs. Tupelo's house should be only two miles down the road. It was going to be a longer trek without the bike, but at least he knew where he was. And more importantly, he was out of the woods. After the wild animals and makeshift distillery, Josh had no desire to see what other secrets the forest or the kudzu held.

Hot and exhausted, Josh flung himself onto his bed. He glanced at the vines that cloaked his room in green and fell asleep to the sounds of the night.

He wasn't sure how long he slept but the chorus of clicking bugs now included chittering birds. When he opened his eyes hints of morning spilled in through the windows.

He jolted up in bed. The kudzu was gone.

The window above the desk was clear and he could see the forest beyond. No green gripped his desk. Josh had forgotten that a window facing the back of the house existed, but there it was, unencumbered, light streaming in. Only the azalea bushes out front blocked the view to the road. No vines to speak of.

Josh swung his legs around, put his feet on the oval braided rug and rubbed his face. He looked all over again. One of the three pictures beside his window tilted askance. Torn leaves lay scattered on the desk. Maybe someone tugged the kudzu out the way it had come in?

Hard sounds of treading across the roof caused him to get up. Josh stumbled over, leaned on the desk, stuck his head out the window and looked up.

"Hello?" he called.

Footsteps clomped to the edge and a thick man with shaggy hair looked down at Josh looking up.

"Morning, you must be Josh. Hope I didn't wake you. This stuff got real outta hand while I was away."

"Are you Mrs. Tupelo's son? Aaron?"

"How'd you know my name was Aaron? Everyone calls me AJ. Ma tell you?" he asked still peering down at Josh.

"No, I figured it out. I've been admiring your artwork, the bluebirds hanging by the desk."

"Man, you're lucky I got her to take down the others." AJ put the clippers down and lifted the front of his shirt to wipe sweat from his face. "Heard you had a hectic few days. How ya holding up?"

Josh thought it over, all of it, "You know, I'm doin' alright."

Josh pulled himself back through the window and looked around the room. It was time to go.

He washed up and grabbed his black duffel bag. As he shut the door behind him he noticed the bright blue tarp had something under it. He pulled the plastic up. The loaner bike. He left it at Wendy's when he bolted last night. She must have dropped it off before work.

Josh gave a quick knock and walked through the open door to the apple yellow kitchen. Mrs. Tupelo leaned forward over the table. Her short curly hair lightly brushed a painted yellow eyed daisy on the hanging lamp. With steady hands, she poured batter into a muffin tin lined with pastel accordion paper cups.

"Josh, if you can wait ten minutes I'll give you some corn muffins to take with you," Mrs. Tupelo offered.

"I'd love to, but I have to go," Josh said. Heavy footfall from above made them both look up.

"Did you meet my son?"

"AJ, yeah I did. We talked a little."

"If you can't wait for muffins there's grits ready on the stove there."

"I gotta get going."

"Well, even if you don't need to spend the night on your way back, you're still welcome to stop in for some sweet tea."

He watched her work a moment and something in his demeanor shifted, "You've always been so nice to me, Mrs. Tupelo."

"You're a good boy," she said, focusing on pouring the fluid dough to the brim of each paper liner.

"I don't know about that," Josh said quite calm. "I made sure to only tell Sheriff Briggs the bare minimum. He doesn't have the full story. Nobody does. I'm the only one who *really* knows what happened in the Edwards house." A cloud must have passed before the sun causing the kitchen to grow darker.

"What do you mean? If you have nothing to hide, why would you do that?" She glanced up at Josh trying to glean some information from his expression.

A smile grew across his face, "Remember when you

took me in? I said no good deed goes unpunished?"

A thud directly overhead caused Mrs. Tupelo to spill muffin batter on the table. AJ must have dropped the clippers. She grabbed her heart, turning her face up, afraid her son might fall through.

She headed over to a tea towel on the oven handle. When Josh saw what she was going for he slipped it off and handed it to her. Her steps slowed on the way back to the table, what Josh said sinking in.

"But why, why would you conceal facts from the law? Or from anyone?" she asked.

"Because of you, Mrs. Tupelo." Josh gripped the chair back and leaned forward to look her directly in the eye. "Mrs. Tupelo, I wanted to give you an exclusive."

14

For the first time Josh passed beneath the 'Irons Stables' archway in his own car instead of Sheriff Briggs' or on the borrowed bike.

Christian hauled burlap bags of feed off the back of a pickup. When he saw Josh he dropped a sack off his shoulder and clapped his hands together back and forth to get off the feed dust. Josh got out and spun his car keys around his finger once before sticking them in his pocket.

"So this is your ride," Christian said. "Finally got it back."

"So you decided to show up to work today," Josh said.

"Watch it you. Gonna miss you, man. Don't be a stranger."

"I'm passing through here on my way back home. I'll see you again. Hey, how'd your date with Wendy go last night?"

"She doesn't like bowling so we went to mini golf."

"Had fun?"

"Had a great time. Glad we went, but don't seem like she's for me."

"Oh, I don't know, she's alright."

"Fine, you want her, you go for her."

Josh gave Christian a slap on the shoulder and said, "Thanks, I might just. See you in a week," before he hopped in his car and drove off.

Josh only met her a couple times, but even from behind and at a great distance, he could tell the redhead by the road was Lou Ann. She had a bounce in her step and Pistachio trotted alongside still wearing Cora Michelle's bow.

"Do you need a lift somewhere?" Josh asked. Lou Ann walked around to his side of the car.

"I thought you'd be long gone with you off the hook and all," Lou Ann said.

"Had to take care of a few things. I'm leaving now, but I'd be happy to drive you where you're going."

"That's thoughtful. But I'm just taking her for a walk."

Josh opened his car door, leaned down and gave the little terrier a scratch behind the ears.

"Pistachio, you're so cute. You're still wearing your bow," he said.

"What do you mean 'still wearing'? Did you put it on her?"

"I don't put bows on dogs." Josh readjusted himself back in his seat and shut the car door.

"How did you know her name?"

"Well..."

"Josh, did you bring my dog back to me?"

"It wasn't me."

"Who then?"

"Sorry, Lou Ann, my lips are sealed. I'm not gonna be the one to ruin his bad boy reputation by letting everyone know he's a good guy."

He gave a parting wave and drove on. He only hung out with one guy here. It wouldn't be hard for her to figure out. Then he thought maybe he didn't help Christian like he should have and threw the car in reverse. Lou Ann heard him coming backwards and waited. Pistachio wagged her tail in anticipation.

"And I think he quit smoking," Josh said quickly before shifting into drive and taking off.

The brass bell on the door jingled as Josh walked into the diner. Except for two empty stools at the counter every seat was taken. He was surprised how many people were there. Crack of dawn must be a busy time in a farming community.

Those who saw him come in stopped talking, wondering why he was still in town and what he was going to do. Others sensing the rolling wave of quiet, looked to see what was going on until rather quickly the whole diner fell silent. Josh tried to hold it together. He looked around, but no Wendy. Was it her day off? He lingered in the center of the diner, not sure what to do with his hands. Then Wendy came from the back with an order of pancakes and placed them in front of Elmer James, the red bearded man, reading the paper on his usual stool.

"Here you go. Enjoy," Wendy said. She looked just like the day he met her, pale blue uniform, short threads of blonde hair working their way out of her ponytail, and that smile. The lack of chatter struck her and she looked up.

Everyone looked. No one felt like waiting to hear

what happened with the boy bandit secondhand. Josh walked over to Wendy with only the red sparkle counter separating them.

"Wendy, can I talk to you outside?" Josh asked.

"Well, I'm in the middle of a shift. What's going on?"

"Uh, I've been thinking about it." He glanced over his shoulder to see all the patrons listening intently, everyone. There was no backing down now. "Come with me to Brooklyn."

"New York?" she said, not sure if he was joking.

"I'll be back this way in a few days. Come with me. You'll love it."

"What do you mean?" Wendy said.

"When I first met you you said you'd never left Mississippi. That this is the only world you've ever known. I'd love to show you something new."

"Josh, this is real sudden."

"I know. I should have left yesterday. The only reason I stayed is you. I don't want to leave without you, Wendy."

"I really like you, Josh. I want to go to Brooklyn and I want to go with you. But I, I don't know. I don't, I don't even have any luggage for my clothes."

"You want to go with me, but you don't have … luggage?" With his whole hand, so as to cover his face for a moment, Josh pushed his dark rimmed glasses up the bridge of his nose. He wished if nothing else someone would stomp around on this roof to break the deafening quiet. "I see," he said. He had not anticipated that answer. It seemed as simple as that. He turned around, walked to the door and left.

As the glass door shut behind him Wendy called out,

"Josh," and took a quick step like she was going to run around the counter after him, but stopped herself. People watched and whispered so she went back to work, taking the coffee pot and refilling low cups at the counter. She stopped pouring to look for Josh and his car through the glass so she could see him drive away.

But Josh wasn't leaving. He was emptying the contents of his black duffle bag into the trunk of his car. The same people who shifted in their seats to watch him go, twisted back around to see what he had to say as he came back in. He dropped the empty black bag on the counter.

"Problem solved," Josh said. Wendy looked around. An older waitress closed her eyes and slowly nodded. "I know this is home, but there's a big world out there. What do you say?" Josh asked.

"If you'll be here again at the end of the week, why don't you take me out on a date? Maybe we can start from there and then you can show me the big wide world?"

"It's a date then," he said with more confidence than he'd had in a long time.

Josh gave a single knock on the counter before he turned. He couldn't take his eyes off Wendy. As he proceeded through the door Clive barged in and the two collided in the doorway.

"Been looking for you," Clive said. Josh didn't want to fight. Especially not in front of Wendy and everyone in the diner.

"Look, Clive--" Josh said putting his hands up.

"--Sheriff said you complained I hadn't been paid by Mrs. Edwards for the work I did over at her place. He went and talked to her. She finally coughed it up, gave me my dough. Guess I owe you a thank you."

Josh opened his mouth to say no need just as Clive

pushed past him and took a seat at the counter.

"Oh, well, good enough," Josh said to no one in particular. He checked the time. A touch behind schedule, but he wanted to make one last quick stop.

Past the church, down the way, Josh parked in the shade. A man out front in a canvas gardening hat and khakis faced the church wall and took no notice of Josh. He watered the white roses that bloomed beneath the blue stained glass windows. When he determined one bush was watered sufficiently he took a side step and water the next.

Josh slipped into the rectory through the double doors. He cautiously situated himself outside the room where he had made the toy and book donations days before. The door rested ajar. He peeked through the gap. Cool air blasted on him from the broken air conditioner. Although it seemed a tight squeeze, Mrs. Tupelo sat at the community quilt with the sewing circle, sewing away. A table beneath supported the center and the edges lay in the members' laps as they worked. All the fabric had been cut in uniform hexagons. The shape and varying shades of bright daffodil, biscuits and blush made him think of a honey hive with the bees hard at work.

Many women of the circle had apparently given up stitching altogether. Two women sat with their eyes fixed on Mrs. Tupelo, their mouths hanging wide open. One woman's extended arm seemed stuck in suspended animation, pulling thread through, but no longer moving. They were all too engrossed in the story.

"The shadow grew on the wall and in the outline Josh thought he saw the stranger holding a rifle," Mrs. Tupelo said.

"A rifle?!" one of the women exclaimed.

"He didn't know what he'd walked in on. Josh said he was so terrified he couldn't run. He stumbled over his own feet and hit the floor. When Mr. Jenkins Senior turned the corner Josh saw that in his hands, he was only holding a broom."

A few of the women gave a sigh of relief.

"What did Josh say then?" Mrs. B. asked, leaning forward, patting her big blonde confection of a hairdo.

"He didn't say anything. He sat there in shock. He was even more shocked when he got invited to stay for dinner."

All the women laughed.

"And then," Mrs. Tupelo continued, but Josh was already on his way out.

He got into his boxy four door, turned the keys in the ignition and the clunker started up. It surprised him how thoroughly he knew the roads here after only a few days. He flipped on the radio, turning the dial to find music he liked. A quick jerk of the wheel to avoid a pothole reminded him what started all this in the first place. He turned off the radio and instead began whistling a little tune.

Josh headed out to Baton Rouge. The thickets and trees covered in a blanket of vines whizzed by. And as he drove farther out, cropland sprawled, the woods and kudzu dropped away and the skies became wide open.

CPSIA information can be obtained
at www.ICGtesting.com
Printed in the USA
FSHW021649221020
75014FS